Stagecoach Surprise

"Hold up!" Slocum shouted. He drew his six-gun and aimed it at the stagecoach guard. "Drop that shotgun! Grab a handful of sky!"

The guard turned and did as he was told. Slocum went cold inside. The man didn't look frightened or angry by being robbed. The smile splitting his face was one of pure triumph. Sunlight glinted off a badge pinned to his shirt and partially hidden by his dusty vest.

Slocum pointed his six-shooter at the passengers, only to find himself staring at three rifles held by three steely eyed deputies . . .

Slocum wasted no time putting his heels to his horse and rocketing away. Bending low, he zigzagged to keep the lawmen's aim off. When he came to the river's edge, he urged his horse across and then up a gentle incline away from the water.

It would have been a decent getaway. But when he got to higher ground, he saw a posse riding up behind the struggling stagecoach. Four men in the posse handed over the reins of riderless horses to the marshal and his three deputies. Now, Slocum had eight men on his trail and nowhere to hide.

JAKE LOGAN

SLOCUM'S
SNAKE OIL

JOVE BOOKS, NEW YORK

THE BERKLEY PUBLISHING GROUP
Published by the Penguin Group
Penguin Group (USA) Inc.
375 Hudson Street, New York, New York 10014, USA
Penguin Group (Canada), 90 Eglinton Avenue East, Suite 700, Toronto, Ontario M4P 2Y3, Canada
(a division of Pearson Penguin Canada Inc.)
Penguin Books Ltd., 80 Strand, London WC2R 0RL, England
Penguin Group Ireland, 25 St. Stephen's Green, Dublin 2, Ireland (a division of Penguin Books Ltd.)
Penguin Group (Australia), 250 Camberwell Road, Camberwell, Victoria 3124, Australia
(a division of Pearson Australia Group Pty. Ltd.)
Penguin Books India Pvt. Ltd., 11 Community Centre, Panchsheel Park, New Delhi—110 017, India
Penguin Group (NZ), 67 Apollo Drive, Rosedale, North Shore 0632, New Zealand
(a division of Pearson New Zealand Ltd.)
Penguin Books (South Africa) (Pty.) Ltd., 24 Sturdee Avenue, Rosebank, Johannesburg 2196,
South Africa

Penguin Books Ltd., Registered Offices: 80 Strand, London WC2R 0RL, England

This is a work of fiction. Names, characters, places, and incidents either are the product of the author's imagination or are used fictitiously, and any resemblance to actual persons, living or dead, business establishments, events, or locales is entirely coincidental.

SLOCUM'S SNAKE OIL

A Jove Book / published by arrangement with the author

PRINTING HISTORY
Jove edition / May 2010

Copyright © 2010 by Penguin Group (USA) Inc.
Cover illustration by Sergio Giovine.

ISBN: 978-0-515-14793-3

JOVE®
Jove Books are published by The Berkley Publishing Group,
a division of Penguin Group (USA) Inc.,
375 Hudson Street, New York, New York 10014.
JOVE® is a registered trademark of Penguin Group (USA) Inc.
The "J" design is a trademark of Penguin Group (USA) Inc.

PRINTED IN THE UNITED STATES OF AMERICA

10   9   8   7   6   5   4   3   2   1

1

"Them horses're gonna be swayback from haulin' that much gold." The man hiccupped loudly and wobbled a bit as he stared at John Slocum through bloodshot eyes.

"Let me get you another drink, old-timer," Slocum said. He motioned to the barkeep, who attentively poured a shot of cloudy, amber tarantula juice into the drained glass in front of the tipsy man.

Slocum's drinking companion reached for the shot glass but missed by an inch and scooted it precariously across the bar. Slocum moved like a striking snake and caught the filled glass before it crashed to the floor. He gently nudged it into the man's grasp. With both hands to steady his aim, the man lifted the glass to his lips, tasted the whiskey in obvious appreciation, and then downed it with a single loud gulp.

He almost fell backward onto the sawdust-covered saloon floor. Slocum grabbed a handful of shirt and kept the man from hurting himself.

"Let's find a chair for you." Slocum snared the whiskey bottle from its spot on the bar as he went. The man clutched his empty glass like a lover. Slocum and the stagecoach agent went through a strange dance, stumbling against each other, staggering, stepping until both were seated at a table in the corner of the long, narrow room. At the rear two of the soiled doves worked to ply their trade but weren't finding any takers. It was a hot night in Fargo, North Dakota, with nary a breeze blowing to carry away the humid air or the sweat beading Slocum's face like tiny diamonds.

He had to admit the sweat came as much from excitement as the sultry weather. Not in Fargo for a day, he had just struck the mother lode of information in the drunken stagecoach agent. For the price of a couple drinks, the man was willing to reveal the deepest, darkest secrets of his company. And what secrets they were!

"Why's the room still spinnin' round?" the agent asked. He clung to table edge as if this kept him from falling upward to the ceiling. Slocum didn't want that happening. There were gaps in the plaster as large as his hand, showing faint stars in the outside sky. No matter what, he didn't want to lose his newest best friend.

"You gents looking for some feminine companionship?" A skinny whore hovered near the table. Her eyes were hot and haunted. Slocum knew the look of a woman taking too much laudanum to kill the boredom and the pain.

"Me and my friend are having a private conversation."

"I kin do you both. A special since it's slow tonight. The pair of you for a dollar."

"Dollar?" The station agent frowned as he worked on the economics of the offer. "I ain't got a dollar, but I got a dime."

"That'll do fer me to do you," she said hastily. Her desperation told Slocum getting rid of her wasn't going to be easy. She needed her drug and even a dime in return for a roll in the hay was a fair price.

Slocum held out his hand to push her back. He pressed his palm into her bony rib cage and fancied he could feel the irregular beating of her drug-infused heart.

"Watch it, mister. You want a feel, you gotta pay for it," she said, glaring at Slocum. "I got me an offer, and I'm an honorable whore. I deliver on the deal. Come on, Slattery. My crib's next door and—"

"And nothing," Slocum said in a voice cold enough to drop the temperature in the room a few degrees. The sharpness of his words froze the woman. She stared at him with a mixture of fear and drug-dulled lust.

"You cain't tell me what to do." Her words were bold but the tone hesitant and almost skittish. Slocum figured she had been knocked around too much to have any confidence left. And he didn't care one whit about her plight. He had his own concerns, and she only derailed them by interrupting like this.

"I just did. Go hustle someone else. Like him." Slocum pointed to a cowboy across the room who eyed them with a mixture of fear and anger. "I reckon that one's sweet on you. He has the look."

"Who?" The cyprian half turned and saw the man Slocum had pointed out. "Oh, that's only Billy Johansson. He don't have two nickels to rub together."

"Might be worth your while to find out. Unless my eyes deceive me, that's a silver dollar riding in his vest pocket."

"Silver?" The woman veered away and headed for Billy. Slocum had seen homing pigeons with less instinct where to go.

"Ain't she gonna stay?" Slattery asked. "Why's she goin' away? I got a dime. Somewhere." He patted himself down, hunting for the furtive coin. "You kin loan it to me. Yer a f-friend. Good f-friend who buys me whiskey and whores." Slattery hiccupped again.

"Don't worry about it," Slocum said. "Not when I'm pouring you another drink. You have the look of a man whose throat is too parched for anything else." He had to be careful about giving Slattery too much. The man could hold his liquor, but Slocum didn't want him passing out. There was no telling how much whiskey Slattery had put away before Slocum came in to wet his own whistle.

"Yer a good man, uh, what's yer name?" Slattery started to slide out of the chair but ran into the wall first. Slocum grabbed him and pulled him upright in the chair—or as upright as he was going to get until he slept off his drunk.

"Call me John."

"Yer a damn fine man, John. Anybody e'er tell you that 'fore?"

"All the time," Slocum lied. "You're a good judge of men."

"I knew it. I kin truss you." Slattery began slurring his words more and fought to keep his eyelids from sinking closed. Slocum clacked the glass on the table like a gunshot to keep Slattery from fading away into a drunken stupor. The station agent's eyes popped open. "Whass that you said?"

"Must be hard, being the only Wells Fargo agent in town. A lot of responsibility."

"Lot. Like that gold shipment," Slattery said. "You won't tell nobody, will you, Josh?"

"No one," Slocum said, telling the absolute truth now. It had been a hard, hungry month riding up from Kansas City. The entire country was locked in a panic and nobody had a job to give him, no matter that he could and would do any honest day's work. That hadn't left a whole lot but the illegal to keep him alive. Petty poaching hardly counted, but the lure of a gold shipment on the stage drew him like flies to fresh cow flop.

"Thought you was honest. You got the look, Joe."

Slocum poured another drink, estimating his chances of getting the information out of Slattery about his gold shipment before the man passed out for the night. As Slattery reached for the full glass, Slocum moved it just out of his shaking grasp.

"When's it going out?"

"Mornin'. Only the usual shotgun guard 'cuz we been robbed so much. Don't wanna make it ob-obvious." Slattery belched loudly. "Tryin' make it all seem like nuthin' more'n mail aboard."

"How many passengers?"

"Don't know. Might not be more'n the two I done sold tickets to. A preacher an' a peddler."

Slocum let the station agent have the drink that pushed him over the edge into complete inebriation. Slattery fell facedown on the table, turned a little, and started snoring. Leaning back, Slocum worked on the information. In spite of Slattery being pop-skull drunk, he believed the story about the gold. A single guard along with the driver, a pair of passengers unlikely to put up much fuss, especially if Slocum let them keep their rings and watches and anything else—it was perfect.

He patted Slattery on the back and said loudly, "Good night, partner. See you in the morning." A quick look around the saloon showed there hadn't been any need for him to go through this little act. The skinny whore and Billy Johansson had disappeared. The other lady of the night was busy on her knees under the table at the rear of the saloon, a look of delight on the cowboy's face. The barkeep argued with two patrons at the bar, and nobody paid Slocum the least bit of attention. He doubted any of them would even remember his face. Slattery certainly wouldn't after he sobered up.

Slocum slipped into the moist night, his head full of plans for the morning.

The land was as flat as a checkerboard, making the robbery a mite more difficult. Slocum had found a spot where the road went down a sharp embankment to cross a shallow stream. No matter how reckless the driver, he had to slow at this point. Water sloshed up over the shanks, forcing his horse to carefully step. Even if the driver knew this was a decent ford, the horses had to slow, and that would be good enough for Slocum to become a road agent again.

He had waited in town to be sure the stagecoach was going to roll at dawn. A peddler slept in a chair on the front porch of the depot. From what Slocum could tell, the gold was secure in the Fargo bank and wouldn't be moved until departure. He considered robbing the guards loading it onto the stage, then knew this was the better plan. A town had marshals and deputies, not to mention citizens passing by who might consider it their civic duty to get involved. Out here on the prairie there'd be only the shotgun guard and the driver to contend with.

From what Slattery had hinted, there would be enough gold in this shipment to let a man eat high on the hog for a year. By then, Slocum knew business would pick up again and he could get a decent job. When even the ranchers began letting their top hands go, it was time to run for the tall grass and let everything settle down.

Or maybe, he thought, it was the right time to stir things up a mite with a stagecoach robbery.

He sat a little straighter in the saddle when he felt a vibration through the hard-packed dirt of the road. Slocum frowned. This was too much disturbance for a stage, even one creaking under a heavy load of gold. Standing in the stirrups, he saw a distant dust cloud rolling along. He settled back down to wait for the stagecoach. A herd of buffalo migrated westward. This might be a problem since he intended to ride in that direction after he stole the shipment. Heading southward might be a better escape, but he discarded the idea. Westward eventually took him into mountains and away from the endless sea of grass where a man stood out for an eternity. He knew that eternity was only about three miles, but if anyone pursued, he wanted somewhere to go to ground.

The Black Hills were a better choice than the prairie for that.

He heard the rattle of harness and the neighing of horses before he saw the stagecoach. Slocum pulled up his bandanna to hide his face, touched the ebony handle of his Colt Navy slung in its cross-draw holster, and settled his mind. This would be over fast. Come at them from the side, take out the guard and driver, load the gold into his saddlebags, maybe cut the team free to strand everyone here by the stream. He played this over and over in his head until the dream hardened into a distinct plan.

The driver snapped his whip to get the team of four horses up the incline to the stream bank. For a moment the horses were on one side of the embankment and the coach on the other. Then the heavy Concord came rolling down as the horses hit the water and slowed.

"Damn you, you worthless varmints. Keep pullin'! I ain't gettin' stuck here again!" The driver cracked his whip above the lead horse's ears, but the animal had its own ideas about how fast to cross the stream.

"Hold up!" Slocum shouted. He drew his six-gun and aimed it at the guard. "Drop that shotgun! Grab a handful of sky!"

The guard turned and did as he was told. Slocum went cold inside. The man didn't look frightened or angry at being robbed. The smile splitting his face was one of pure triumph. As the guard turned, sunlight glinted off a badge pinned to his shirt and partially hidden by his dusty vest.

Slocum twisted and pointed his six-shooter at the passengers, only to find himself staring at three rifles poking out through the windows. He didn't recognize the peddler's face behind any of those rifles—only steely-eyed deputies. He fired, spooking the horses. They kicked up froth from the river and tried to bolt. Slocum began firing steadily, one slug ripping through the thin wooden door and finding a home in one of the lawmen. The loud yelp of pain told that it wasn't a serious wound but enough to cause some consternation inside the coach.

When his Colt came up empty, Slocum wasted no time turning his pony's face and putting his heels to heaving flanks. The horse rocketed away, spurred on by the lead flying through the air all around. Slocum winced as a hot sting touched his leg. He glanced down and saw a shallow groove cut through his jeans. Blood oozed out but was more annoying than dangerous since it had barely broken the skin.

Bending low, he zigzagged to keep the lawmen's aim off. When he got closer to the stream, he urged his horse across. It was a risky move since the horse began high stepping through the deep water, but the marshal was having trouble with his trap, too. The men inside the coach tried to climb out and got in each other's way. When the marshal stood in the driver's box, rifle to his shoulder, the team surged forward and threw him off balance, causing his round to sail high over Slocum's head.

Then Slocum was across the stream and galloping his horse up a gentle incline away from the stream and across the prairie. It would have been a decent getaway, but when he got to higher ground he saw a posse riding up behind the struggling stagecoach. Four men in the posse handed over the reins of riderless horses to the marshal and his deputies from the stage. Slocum had eight men on his trail and nowhere to hide.

"Three miles," he grunted, hunkering down low as he kept his horse galloping. That was how far the lawmen could see him on flat land. Slocum might have seen more level prairie in his day, but he couldn't remember when.

It meant that pursuit was going to be easy.

When his horse began to tire, Slocum had to slow. A quick glance over his shoulder showed the posse far behind, but the marshal was a shrewd man and this obviously was not his first pursuit. He held his men back to maintain a steady gait so he could follow all day and never flag. Slocum walked his horse to give it a rest, then brought it to a canter. His best chance for escape lay in varying his pace, keeping the horse from dying under him, and maybe something would rescue him.

Slocum saw no way but blind luck out of this predicament.

He cursed himself for being so gullible. Slattery had been a plant. If Slocum had been more cautious, he would have learned about the marshal and how he operated. A drunk station agent spouting "secret" information had been too good for Slocum to pass up, having just drifted into town. And to top it off he had bought a half bottle of whiskey to pour down Slattery's gullet. Somehow, that irked him almost as much as falling for a transparent trap.

"It was the peddler sleeping on the boardwalk," he decided. The peddler had given an air of authenticity to everything Slattery had said. If he had been more careful in planning, he would have watched who climbed aboard at the Fargo depot and would have seen they carried rifles.

There was no time to cry over spilled milk. Slocum detoured down a shallow ravine cut through the prairie by endless hours of wind and heavy storm, hoping to drop out of sight. His head bobbed up over the edge of the wash and he saw how the marshal had accurately followed the dodge. His predicament was even more dire than before. The lawman had spread his posse out in a fan pattern, a couple heading to a spot that would soon be far behind Slocum's trail, to keep him from backtracking. The rest were aimed either for him or ahead, in the direction he traveled. If he stayed in the ravine too long, he would find himself staring up at deputies aiming rifles along the banks.

The dirt walls were crumbly and didn't afford anywhere for Slocum to get out. He urged his horse to a quicker pace. If he stayed in this rut, it would quickly turn into his grave. For the marshal to lay such a trap showed how seriously he took stagecoach robbery. Slattery might not have been joshing about there being a lot of thefts if the marshal could put such a large posse onto the trail of a solitary road agent.

"Was there even any gold? Why didn't I ask where it was headed? Who was shipping it?" A dozen other questions worried at Slocum like a burr under his saddle blanket, but this self-flagellation was only a way to keep from thinking about the posse closing in on him. He hadn't asked the right questions and now had to live with the result—or die from it.

A gully cut into the deeper ravine, giving Slocum the chance to cut off at an angle away from the posse. His horse struggled to get up the soft dirt bank, and then he found himself heading due north with the lawmen on the far side of the ravine. It wasn't much of a barrier, but it would slow them a little.

Two bullets sang past him, both too high. From the distance came the cry "Give up! Surrender and we won't gun you down."

Slocum sneered at this. All it meant was that the marshal knew where a tree with limbs strong enough for a hanging grew on the prairie. That would save him and his deputies a few bullets. Giving up now was out of the question if Slocum wanted to keep sucking in the humid North Dakota air for even another day.

With a sudden shift in direction, he avoided a new fusillade from behind. The posse was getting closer but still out of range. Slocum had been a sniper during the war, and even he would have had a difficult time hitting a galloping target on horseback at three hundred yards while on horseback himself.

As he rode, his heart skipped a beat. The riders were almost on top of him. He looked back, sure he was done for. He frowned when he realized that the marshal and his deputies weren't any closer, but the vibration coming up from the ground equaled a herd of horses.

Or a herd of buffalo.

Slocum risked standing in the stirrups and saw the buffalo herd he had spotted earlier now milling about uneasily. The herd was upset over the rifle shots but so far didn't smell any humans close enough to cause worry. If the posse had been buffalo hiders, they could have used tripods and rifles powerful enough to drop a bull at twice this distance.

A million thoughts flashed through Slocum's head. He wasn't even aware he had come to a decision as he sawed at the reins and sent his horse directly for the buffalos. They were stupid beasts that acted instinctively. Any threat caused them to stampede.

And John Slocum rode directly into them.

The stampede began, with him smack in the middle of thousands of tons of frightened buffalo.

2

The woolly behemoths stirred and then began to run, stumbling along at first and then finding their balance to race across the prairie hard. Slocum knew that he would be dead in an instant if his horse faltered. A misstep would send both of them crashing to the ground under the flashing hooves of the now-terrified buffaloes. His horse tried to veer away from the herd, but Slocum held it in a direct line where he could ride among the leaders in the rampaging herd.

The thunder grew and deafened him. Dust rose and clogged his nose and blinded him. He pulled up his bandanna again, but this time he needed it just to breathe. He clung fiercely to the reins and pressed his knees into his horse for as much support as possible. He might die here, stomped into bloody oblivion by a thousand buffaloes, not even leaving behind much more than a wet smear on the prairie, but this was preferable to getting strung up by the posse now far behind him.

What seemed an eternity passed, and Slocum grew woozy from the dust clogging his nose and mouth, and then he snapped alert. His horse began limping, just a little. Slowing in the middle of the herd spelled immediate death, but the horse could not keep up the breakneck pace. Slocum used every bit of his skill, bouncing off the sides of struggling buffaloes like a billiard ball caroming around a table, forcing his horse to keep running until he could find a pace that let the buffaloes slip past without crashing into them. Bit by bit he fell back in the herd and eventually popped out the rear, the deadly flashing hooves ahead of him.

Slocum pulled the bandanna down off his face and squinted. He was still cloaked by the dust cloud and had to make the best use of this before the marshal came looking for his body. Not sure what direction he rode, he angled away with the herd's crashing sounds on his right. This kept him moving away from the posse—he hoped.

When he finally rode clear of the dust, he saw that the buffaloes had added another mile to the distance between him and his pursuers. To his surprise he found he trotted along a road showing evidence of considerable recent traffic. Craning around, he studied the back trail for sign of the posse. Starting a buffalo stampede had bought him time, and if luck held as it had so far, the marshal would simply give up and go back to Fargo, to continue his hunt for other outlaws intent on robbing the stagecoach.

A rifle report in the distance brought Slocum up short. He strained to hear a second shot, but it never came. He unknotted his bandanna to remove it from his gritty neck and snapped it a few times to get the dust off. Every move he made caused a small dust cloud to hang around him. He tried to bring his horse to a trot, but the animal balked. Slocum dismounted and led his horse a few paces, watching the front right leg. The soreness wasn't too bad, but if he pushed the pace any more, the horse would pull up lame. Being stranded when a posse was hot on his trail didn't appeal to Slocum.

Another shot caused him to reach for his six-shooter. His

hand lingered on the butt for a moment before he remembered the cylinder was empty. He let his horse rest while he reloaded. A third rifle report from the direction of the posse caused him to load all six chambers. Usually, he rode with the hammer resting on an empty chamber to prevent a jolt from causing an unwanted discharge, but he knew he would need as many bullets as possible if the lawmen caught up with him.

A fourth shot made him wonder what was going on. He let his horse continue walking along the road while he climbed a small rise that was hardly a bump in the prairie. The elevation gave him a hint of what lay behind him. A larger dust cloud to the far north showed where the buffaloes had finally gone, but the smaller cloud had to be kicked up by the posse. He estimated they were only a couple miles behind him. The herd would have hidden his tracks, but if the marshal refused to believe he had no chance of finding his quarry, the posse would hunt until they either deserted and went home or the marshal found the trail.

Another rifle report made Slocum worry that the posse was trying to flush him by firing into brush. That meant they knew he wasn't dead.

Whether they believed this or the marshal just refused to go back to Fargo without his quarry didn't matter. They were still after him. Slocum slipped back down the low hill and caught up with his horse. The limp was more pronounced now and the flesh tender to the touch.

"There, there, old girl," Slocum said, gentling the mare. "I'll hoof it so you won't have my weight making that leg worse." He muttered to himself as he took the reins and began walking. The sprain wasn't too bad, but it needed tending. On foot, he was easy prey for the posse.

He followed the road another half mile and then saw wagon tracks cutting across the prairie. Without any idea where the main route led, other than that it went westward, he had no reason to slavishly continue. Slocum led the horse off the deep double-rut road and followed the tracks left by what must have been a small wagon train. There were few trackers more capable than John Slocum, but he couldn't make out how many wagons were in the train. Four men on horseback had ridden on either side, but Slocum guessed there were at least six heavy wagons.

By twilight, Slocum was feeling uneasy about the posse on his trail. He jumped at every sound, and when the dull clop-clop of horses' hooves sounded, his hand flashed to his six-shooter.

"That you, Pa?"

The voice was that of a young boy. Slocum relaxed as a draft horse came out of the dark. Seated on the ponderous horse was a child of six or seven.

"Reckon not," Slocum said. "My horse is going lame, and I followed the wagon tracks. They belong to your wagon?"

"Who are you?"

"Name's Slocum."

"You ain't with us. Pa told me not to talk to strangers, not after what happened back in Illinois."

"I don't mean any harm. And I haven't seen your pa. He out hunting?"

The small, shadowy form shook in such a way that Slocum thought the boy had nodded. Without a moon and with thick clouds hiding most of the starry blanket above, the night was almost like being trapped in a windowless room.

"I haven't heard any gunfire." Slocum lied since he had heard the posse's rifles, but that had been earlier.

"We thought we did, too," the boy said. "That's why I'm worried about my pa."

"You think he had a hunting accident?"

"Might be them that chased us out of town comin' after us."

Slocum figured out what was happening. The wagons

were filled with religious refugees. It didn't matter what sect, though he suspected they might be Mormons. The story of how Brigham Young had founded Salt Lake City was well known.

"If you'll tend my horse, I can go find your pa."

"Ma wouldn't like that. She's worse'n Pa about strangers after what they done to her."

"Your call," Slocum said. He turned and tugged his horse's reins to continue on after the tracks left by the wagons.

"You gonna get shot if you barge in without bein' announced," the boy said. "You better look for the doctor's wagon. He ain't likely to shoot you, no matter how cranky he gets."

"Doctor? People doctor or vet?"

"Reckon he's a people doctor, though Pa says different. Says he's the devil's disciple, but he's not so bad. Gave me candy." There was a tiny gasp, then, "Don't tell my pa that. He don't like me eatin' candy. Says it's Satan's way of lurin' me astray."

"He doesn't like you talking to the doctor, either," Slocum said. "What's the doctor's name?"

"Doc Jerrold, but he told me a secret. That's not his real name."

"So much for keeping a secret," Slocum said, grinning. He wished he could see the boy's face.

"Oh, it ain't *that* kind of secret. Said he uses it as a stage name, but I don't know exactly what that means."

A sharp report caused Slocum to grab for his six-shooter. A bullet ricocheted off into the night after hitting a nearby rock.

"That must be my pa," the boy said. "I better go fetch him."

"You better get on back to your ma," Slocum said. "He's likely to mistake you for game in the dark."

"He couldn't hit the broad side of a barn if he was

locked inside," the boy said. "That's what the other men say. Pa wanted to show 'em wrong."

"I don't think he bagged dinner," Slocum said. "That bullet hit a rock, not a rabbit."

The boy hesitated, then said, "If you follow me, I'll show you to Doc Jerrold's camp. It's a ways from ours."

"Much obliged, but I don't want you getting into hot water with your ma."

"She won't know. She's feelin' poorly."

"Might be Dr. Jerrold could help her."

The boy made a choking sound that Slocum thought was a combination of a laugh and the attempt to stifle it.

He walked his horse behind the boy astride his draft horse. As they went down a gradual incline toward a stream, he saw the dark outlines of a dozen wagons pulled into a circle to pen up their livestock.

"Yonder," the boy said, pointing. Slocum saw a lone wagon twenty yards distant.

"Much obliged." Slocum started toward the outcast wagon.

"Mister," the boy said hesitantly. "Don't say nuthin' to the doctor how I gave away his secret."

"I can keep a secret," Slocum said. "You should, too."

The boy nodded, snapped the horse's reins, and trotted off toward the circled wagons, yelling for his ma to let him inside.

Slocum led his mare over to Dr. Jerrold's wagon and stopped a few yards away to let the man recognize that he had a visitor.

"Who are you?" The question came from Slocum's left, from the direction of the stream. Slocum hadn't even heard the man coming up because the murmuring water masked the sounds of movement.

"A man needing help with his horse. Leg's banged up a mite, but some liniment will fix her up nicely."

"Why you think I can help?"

"You're Dr. Jerrold?"

"Course I am. Either that or I drive an ugly-ass wagon with that name painted on the side for no good reason."

"Then you must have liniment. That's all I want. I can pay for your services."

"I'm not a vet. This is Dr. Josiah Jerrold's Medicine Show, not Dr. Josiah Jerrold's Traveling Veterinary Surgery."

"You peddle medicine? Something you sell must be useful as liniment."

"You must have caught my show back in Bismarck," Jerrold said, hobbling up. Slocum got a better look at the man. Jerrold was in his sixties, with only a faint halo of white hair remaining on his head. Strangely, his eyebrows were bushy black and grew together, making it look as if he had a large furry caterpillar wiggling across his craggy face. The sharp, long nose had been broken and improperly reset more than once. That went along with a white scar on his cheek that caught what little light there was in the dark night and seemed to glow. He approached Slocum. Even when he was standing straight as a ramrod, the top of Jerrold's head hardly came to Slocum's shoulder.

"What? You don't think I look like a doctor? Well, sir, I am a bona fide doctor with degrees from Harvard and the Sorbonne. That's in France."

"Heard tell," Slocum said, grinning. He tried to remember if he had ever heard of a snake oil salesman who didn't claim medical degrees from the most prestigious universities in the world. Who could ever gainsay them when most folks never graduated from high school?

You are a skeptic, sir." Jerrold chuckled. "Good. It shows you are a man of some discernment, if not erudition. I've never been farther east than Columbus, Ohio. Come on. Let's see what I can do for that horse of yours."

Slocum unsaddled the horse and dropped his gear away from the wagon. As he walked back, he saw the gaudy banner on the side of the wagon: "Dr. Josiah Jerrold's Medicine Show." He shook his head in wonder. Folks could be talked into believing about anything. Still, most patent medicines were in large part alcohol, so they did no real harm and actually allowed men prohibited from drinking by their wives a chance to take a nip and call it tonic.

"Don't think it's too bad," Jerrold said, running his gnarled hand over the injured leg with surprising gentleness. The mare whinnied but didn't show any real discomfort. "A drop or two of my special elixir on a rag wrapped around this fine leg ought to fix the little lady up."

Josiah Jerrold set about doing just that, taking a bottle from his coat pocket and splashing some of the thick, yellowish fluid onto a rag. It took him a few minutes to complete the bandage, but Slocum's mare stood easy and seemed no worse for the crude veterinary work.

"Much obliged," Slocum said. "What do I owe you?"

Jerrold waved away the offer and held out his bottle, the same he had used to get the potion for the horse's leg.

"Have a toot," he said. "It's not fit for man nor beast, so I use it to kill the pain in both."

Slocum took a swig and rocked back. He had swallowed some vile concoctions in his day, but this was about the most powerful. He handed the bottle back. Jerrold took a long drink, then popped the cork back in and finally wiped his lips on his sleeve.

"Won't kill you or the horse," he promised. "My granddaddy used to make moonshine and taught me all there was to learn. I can make liquor out of anything that'll ferment and some things that won't. You ever had any onion wine? No. Don't. It tastes like piss. Worse. But I've made it and a whole lot more in my day."

"How'd you come to be traveling with the likes of them?" Slocum jerked his thumb over his shoulder in the direction of the other wagons.

"Chance, nothing more. We were all in Bismarck at the

same time. It's not safe for a single wagon to roll through this country. I know. I've done it and barely survived to brag on being so goddamn stupid." Jerrold perched on the lowered gate of his wagon, his bowed legs swinging beneath him. They didn't even touch the ground.

"Who are they?"

"Nobody to fool with, if you've got a mind to," Jerrold said. "Religious folk who actually live what they preach." He shook his head sadly. "I tried to sell them a bottle or two for what ails them, but their leader wouldn't permit it." He chuckled and added, "Usually the offer of a sample to the leader's good enough to open the wallets, but not this time. He refused."

"That's a mite out of the ordinary," Slocum allowed. They said nothing for a spell, sitting in the darkness and listening to the night sounds. In the distance a lonely wolf howled. Slocum thought there was an answer but couldn't be sure. He looked up at the overcast sky.

"Clouds won't go on their way," Jerrold said. "Won't rain, won't let the sun shine. I hate North Dakota."

"Where you heading?"

"West. Don't have a destination in mind. Why burden myself unduly?" He fumbled in his pocket and drew out the bottle of patent medicine again and offered it to Slocum.

Slocum hesitated, then accepted. It was likely the only alcohol he was going to get for a very long time. The botched stagecoach robbery and almost being trampled by a herd of buffalo had caused aches and pains to grow he had ignored for a long time. The burn all the way down to his belly drove off some of those accumulated miseries.

"I ran into a youngster out looking for his pa."

"That'd be Joshua. Not sure of his last name since his folks won't let me talk to him or any of the other children. Can't blame them. Why, I might spirit them away and force them into a nomadic life of seeing what the world has to offer while peddling my patented elixir." Jerrold took another drink. This time he didn't offer more to Slocum, since he finished the bottle down to the last drop.

"He was worried his father would come to harm out hunting. Is his pa that inept?"

Jerrold thought on the matter and finally said, "He's burdened with a load of guilt that he's not as good as he might be. Not sure any man could live up to his personal expectations."

"His or his preacher's?"

"More like his woman. She's a piece of work. Bitter, she is, and never satisfied. I learned a long time back to size up people. Don't think she's smiled once, at least not since she discovered sex. She has the look of a woman who considers the wifely duties to be a . . . chore."

A rifle shot echoed through the still night. Slocum was on his feet immediately, his Colt Navy half-drawn. He held his head turned slightly to pick up the most distant sound. Realizing the picture he made, he looked at Josiah Jerrold and the way the snake oil salesman eyed him.

"Yes, sir, I learned to size up people fast. You don't look like the nervous type, but that gunshot spooked you."

"What do you make of that?" Slocum asked.

Jerrold ran his tongue around his lips as he contemplated how to answer. When he did, it came slow and thoughtful. "You've got enemies."

Slocum looked out into the darkness to see a man tramping back doggedly to the ring of wagons with a large carcass draped over one shoulder and a rifle resting on the other.

"That must be Joshua's pa," he said.

"It is, but who are the others?" Josiah Jerrold pointed into the pitch-black night.

Slocum swung around, his six-shooter cocked and aimed, when the riders came up behind the hunter. He couldn't be sure, but he thought there were eight—and one sported a marshal's badge on his coat lapel.

3

Slocum jerked away and took a step back when Jerrold grabbed his wrist to keep him from swinging around his six-shooter to train it on him.

Slocum locked eyes with the man and saw nothing there to worry over.

"I'd best hit the trail," Slocum said.

"Hide your gear inside the wagon," Jerrold said. "I will handle this, if it needs handling. No need for lead to fly, now is there? My medicine cures what ails you, but it ain't worth shit on bullet wounds."

Slocum considered his options and they were few. His horse had its leg wrapped in the liniment Josiah Jerrold passed off as medicine for humans. There hadn't been enough time for the medication to soak into the ligaments and work out the soreness. The marshal and his posse would have him run to ground within minutes. An even worse solution than running for it was shooting it out. Slocum didn't know the settlers, but he had no quarrel with them. A stray bullet, especially from a trigger-happy posse, was likely to do some damage to livestock or humans.

He slammed his Colt back into the holster, grabbed his saddle, and heaved it up onto the back stage of Jerrold's wagon. He spun about, got inside, and dragged his gear behind a dark curtain that hid the interior. Inside, Jerrold had a laboratory suitable for any respectable town pharmacist. Cabinets of chemicals lined either side of the wagon, and a small bench showed where Jerrold formulated his devil's potion.

Slocum slid his saddle all the way to the front of the wagon and dropped a blanket over it, then sank down next to the workbench and curled up as small as possible. Drawing his legs to his chest made him invisible if anyone poked his head in the back. Or at least Slocum hoped that was true.

He drew his six-gun and held it loosely, listening hard for sounds that Jerrold was betraying him to the marshal for whatever reward might be offered. He heard nothing for a long time, then slow hoofbeats as several horses approached.

"Evening," came the authoritative voice. "I'm the federal marshal for this territory. You see a lone rider in the past few hours?"

"I been camped with the settlers. You already spoke to them?"

"I have, sir. They claimed not to have seen anyone. You know if that rider I'm looking for might have joined up with them?"

"Not likely. They're religious folks and keep to themselves pretty much. That's why they exiled me out here. They don't cotton much to me selling my patent medicines. Tell me, Marshal, you aching from your long ride? I've got just the thing to ease the pain of long travel and make you feel like a youngster again."

"You see any strangers out on the road?"

"No, I haven't. Now, for only one dollar you can cure what ails you with Dr. Josiah Jerrold's Elixir of Health.

Now, I know that's not what the label says. The label says 'Dr. Josiah Jerrold's Extraordinary Tonic,' but the elixir is a new formulation I'm experimenting with and you will be the first—"

"You haven't seen anyone at all?"

"Only the good people in the wagon train. Now, I understand that times are tough. They don't call it a bank panic for no reason. I'll make you a deal. Two bottles of the fine elixir for one dollar. A silver cartwheel in exchange for a week of good health. Is that too much to ask? I don't think it is. Now, would your men enjoy some of my curative, also?"

Slocum grinned as he heard Jerrold continue with his spiel. Then he stiffened, hand clutching the butt of his six-shooter, when he heard boots clacking on the rear platform. It was too dark inside for any light to come through, but he heard the curtain pulled back and someone stepping into the doctor's apothecary.

"Ain't nobody here, Marshal. Just a shitload of smelly chemicals." The deputy came deeper into the wagon and began opening bottles. The odors rose, mingled into something indescribably vile, and made Slocum a little light-headed.

Slocum dared not move. His nose began to twitch as he fought down a sneeze. If he gave himself away now, he'd have the lawmen on his neck so fast he wouldn't be able to take a new breath.

The sound of footsteps came closer. Slocum peered out around the edge of the worktable and saw the toe of a boot. He put his thumb on the six-gun's hammer and almost drew it back. The sound of his six-shooter cocking would alert the man. The deputy was too close not to hear. Slocum wondered how the lawman could be this close and not sense the presence of imminent death.

"Nuthin' here, Marshal."

"Then get your ass out here. We've got more tracking to do."

"In the dark? We ain't got lanterns. How are we supposed . . ." The words trailed off as the deputy left the wagon and continued his complaint outside. Slocum buried his face in the crook of his arm and sneezed. The muffled sound rang like a gunshot in his ears, but none of the posse overheard. Within a minute, the sound of horses trotting away diminished and finally faded to nothing. Only the soft snap of the curtains in a growing breeze greeted his ears. He strained and heard the cattle penned up by the wagons and possibly the murmur of the nearby stream. The posse had ridden away.

He jumped a foot when Jerrold suddenly appeared over him. The doctor had entered so quietly Slocum had not heard, and he had been listening hard.

"You move like an Apache," Slocum said.

"Put that hogleg away. The marshal's gone on his way with his boorish crew." Jerrold sank down on a crate and stared at Slocum. In the dark his eyes took on a curious glow, as if he were some Halloween jack-o'-lantern lit up from inside.

"You didn't have to hide me. You took quite a risk."

"Let's say my previous dealings with the law have been less than salubrious."

Slocum said nothing.

"That means they weren't healthful," Jerrold said sharply. "I don't like the jackasses wearing those badges and thinking they're so much better'n everybody else. They do nothing but overcharge me for sales permits, then run me out of town when it suits their purpose. More than once they've stolen every dime I made. Fines, they say. Robbery, I say!"

"Thanks." Slocum painfully unwound himself from the tight cubbyhole where he had hidden. Unable to stand to his full height, he bent over the worktable.

"Can you stopper up those bottles? The stench is making me sick to my stomach."

"Ah, yes, I forget how such rare chemicals might affect

the uninitiated." Jerrold pushed past Slocum and dexterously closed the bottles, then returned them to their proper spots on the shelf. Slocum saw that the wood shelves had holes drilled in them so the bottles fit snugly and would not bounce around as Jerrold drove his wagon over rough roads.

"That's a clever arrangement. What else have you done to the wagon?" Slocum asked. He ran his finger around one hole to show what he meant.

"I am only a humble entrepreneur, a poor vendor of miraculous elixirs to cleanse the body and ease the mind. I leave the soul cleaning to my holy brothers of the cloth."

Slocum looked at Jerrold and frowned. The man did go on.

"Yes," Jerrold said, "I do enjoy the sound of my own voice. I have traveled alone for so long, it is my only companion. Why, on some days, even my shadow abandons me."

"You might get a dog."

"Yes, my boy, I might." There was a note of longing in Jerrold's voice.

"You had one but he died?" Slocum asked.

"That is so. I called him Buckshot. He was the mangiest dog you have ever seen. Most animals of his species show traces, no matter how faint, of their heritage. He was a breed so mixed he was unique unto himself."

Slocum didn't bother asking what had happened to Buckshot. It didn't matter, and he was anxious to be on his way. But with the federal marshal still hot on his trail, he wasn't likely to go anywhere for a spell. With his horse pulling up lame, it might be a week before he could figure out how to get the hell out of North Dakota.

"I can't pay much," Jerrold said unexpectedly.

"How's that?"

"I need an assistant. A man of your caliber would be ideal to protect me from the ruffians who wear badges and claim to represent the people."

"You want to hire me as a bodyguard?"

"That seems a bit extreme, but yes."

"I'm not a hired gun."

"Nor do I wish you to be. There is no one I want gunned down. I require only small help with the wagon and team and perhaps assistance setting up my show in the next town."

"Where's that likely to be?"

Jerrold rubbed his chin, eyed Slocum appraisingly as if deciding how much he could stretch the truth, then said, "Sentinel Butte. It is three days down the road."

"I'd be gone in four?"

"If that was your choice. I can only pay a dollar a day, but for that you'd have to drive the wagon."

"While you sleep back here?"

Jerrold laughed in delight. "No, my dear boy, not at all. I would require the time to manufacture more of my famous potion, whatever I'd call it this time."

"I see you have a small hand press. You make your own labels?"

"Of course I do. Most of the cretins in the towns I pass through could not spell any of the names correctly." Jerrold snorted and shook his head. "The world is a sorry place, indeed, when a man has to do everything himself."

"You're the doctor," Slocum said. Jerrold laughed and slapped Slocum on the shoulder.

"You have a wit about you. Now let's get some sleep. It is going to be early, perhaps before dawn, when the wagons will pull out. We should be with them."

Slocum nodded, and Jerrold chased him out of the wagon. Slocum took his blanket and considered curling up under the wagon but decided to do some scouting first. He hiked to the road and carefully examined the tracks the best he could. The clouds had blown away, giving ample starlight to study the trail. From all he could tell, the posse had ridden off in the direction to be taken by the wagon train.

Slocum had never even heard of Sentinel Butte, but that wasn't too surprising. Towns popped up and died like weeds. If the town was deep enough into the Black Hills, it might be a mining town. Boomtowns swelled overnight with the influx of miners, and a new strike elsewhere deflated the population just as fast.

Slocum hiked back to the wagon and stopped when he saw a dark figure moving silently away from the circle of wagons. He slipped his pistol from his holster and followed the shadow to the river.

"Who's there?"

Slocum recognized the voice and slid his pistol back into his holster.

"Just me. The man you met earlier," Slocum said to the boy. "Your pa bag enough for dinner?"

"I suppose," the boy said. Slocum moved closer. The boy sat on a rock by the river, knees pulled up and arms around them.

"Something wrong?"

"I don't want to go with my family," the boy said tearfully. "I want to go with Dr. Jerrold."

"Why do you want to run away from your family?" Slocum asked.

"They're boring. Dr. Jerrold's funny. I like him. And he said he'd teach me chemistry. I could mix up stuff, and he could sell it to the marks."

"He tell you that?"

"I overheard him talking to my pa. Pa doesn't like him. But I do."

"Sometimes boring is good," Slocum said. His life had been anything but dull, and at times he wished it had been nice and quiet, that he had settled down and worked as a farmer. He would have, too, if it hadn't been for a carpetbagger judge deciding he wanted to steal away Slocum's Stand back in Calhoun, Georgia. Slocum had returned to Slocum's Stand to recuperate from a bullet in the gut. His parents had died and his brother Robert had been killed during Pickett's Charge, leaving him the sole owner of a fine farm.

He pressed his fingers into the circular lump in his vest pocket. This was his brother's watch—his only legacy. Even this was more than he had gotten from his parents. No taxes had been paid, the carpetbagger judge had claimed. When he and a hired gun rode out to seize the farm, they had bitten off more than they could chew.

Slocum had left their bodies in shallow graves down by the springhouse and had ridden out, never looking back. It was just as well he had ridden fast and far, because a wanted poster for judge killing had followed him ever since. Some men deserved killing, and the greedy judge had been one of them. The law didn't see it that way.

"The law," Slocum said softly, thinking of the marshal on his trail. He had stepped into a bear trap when he tried to rob the stage.

"How's that?" The boy stirred, stretched his legs, and then curled back into a tight ball perched on the slippery rock.

"Nothing," Slocum said. "I was just reflecting how boring can be mighty good. Too much excitement can be the death of you."

"You don't look like a boring guy," the boy said. "That why the doc is letting you ride with him?"

"Who said I was going with Jerrold?"

"I hear things."

"You need to keep that a secret," Slocum said. "Better than you did before."

"Let me go with you and the doctor. Please. I can make myself useful. I can pay my way by working. I'm a hard worker!"

Slocum drew his six-shooter in one smooth move, cocked it, and thrust the muzzle into the boy's face. He yelped and fell back, arms and legs flailing. He recovered himself and stared up with fright-wide eyes.

"Why'd you go and do that?"

"To show you what it's like not being boring. Think of this happening when you least expect it, only the man with the gun pulls the trigger."

"You'd've killed me if you'd fired!"

"Boring can be good," Slocum said, lowering the hammer and slipping the six-shooter back into the holster. He turned and walked off, thinking on ways he could turn his own life into sheer boredom.

With the posse hunting him, he didn't see how that would ever happen.

4

"I don't suppose they think of it as shunning," Josiah Jerrold said, "but that's what it is." He pointed ahead to the last of the settlers' wagons. No matter how fast he drove the medicine wagon, they always kept a respectable distance away from him.

"Reckon they've got their reasons."

"Been thrown out of some fine towns, from what they say. How much of that was not fitting in and standing apart is a question that begs an answer. No one likes to get preached at if all they want's a long drink of clear water."

"You preach to anyone who'll come close enough," Slocum said, grinning crookedly. "The way you tried to peddle your witch's brew to the posse showed that."

"Hell and damnation, boy, that was the only way to get them to leave. They'd still be poking around hunting for you if I hadn't gone into my pitch." Jerrold turned his shiny bald spot around just right to reflect a ray of sunlight into Slocum's eyes. "What do they want you for?"

Slocum twisted away to get the brightness out of his eyes and look forward. In the rear of the wagon sat the boy who had wanted to run away and join Dr. Jerrold peddling his witch's brew in exotic towns—any town was exotic if all you knew was wherever your pa took you. Even at this distance Slocum saw the wistful expression on the boy's face. He wondered if he shouldn't have kept quiet and let Jerrold deal with him, but if he had, Jerrold might have a new assistant. Slocum wouldn't put it past Josiah Jerrold to take in a runaway from a religious sect and think he had done something righteous.

"Does it matter?"

"Of course not. I got the law after me in a dozen towns, but mostly for fraud. They simply did not understand that the power of my elixir sometimes takes several bottles to manifest itself." Jerrold fell silent for a while and then asked, "Robbery? I heard tell that the marshal was fed up with so many stages getting held up and was planning a decoy."

"I wish I'd met you in Fargo," Slocum said. That brought a heartfelt laugh to Jerrold's lips.

He quieted when he saw the wagons ahead veering away off the road to bypass Sentinel Butte.

"Reckon they want to avoid the town on their way to wherever they're going," said Jerrold.

"You talk to the boy about joining you as an apprentice chemist?"

"He had a knack for mixing powders and potions, he did," Jerrold said, nodding, "but I never encouraged him to leave his family. He will one day, and maybe not so far off. I could have used the help, but he was wrong for it."

"You afraid his pa would come after you?"

"His pa?" Jerrold laughed again. "He tries to be a man, but it's the boy's mama I'd worry over. His pa is a terrible hunter, but his mama, now, I'd worry she'd cut my throat while I slept. I had a wife like that once. Just once, mind you, just once."

They watched the wagons angle away from the road and head due south. In a few minutes the road curled about to the northwest and Slocum lost sight of the other wagons entirely. He wished them all well, especially the boy. He recognized the wanderlust in him, the need to find something better and throw off shackles that weren't of his own making. Jerrold was right. The boy wouldn't be with his family much longer. A year, two, then he would quietly leave one night and find his own way.

Slocum wished him well.

"When we get to town, you won't be seen with me. I'll set up the show, then you mosey on over like you were attracted to my spiel and be skeptical about my claims."

"I buy a bottle and am cured?"

"No, no, even yokels in Sentinel Butte won't buy that. Your complaint's minor. You have any idea what they do to keep the town alive?"

Slocum shook his head. "Might be mining."

"Silver mining's my guess. You're a miner with aches. Maybe a slight cough. The elixir cures them. Nothing too spectacular."

"More people are likely to have aches than broken legs?"

"Something like that," Jerrold said, eyeing Slocum sideways. "You sure you never did this before? You have a feel for the con."

"It doesn't take much to figure out what's being sold and how good it is as medicine."

"I'm hoping there's not a doctor in town. They always show up and get nosey unless I've bought them off first."

"You can sell your liniment to cure game horses," Slocum said. His horse walked alongside the wagon without a trace of a limp. Slocum didn't want to try out that leg with a hard gallop, but he thought the mare could support his weight if he wanted to move along. And he would, after Jerrold finished with the citizens of Sentinel Butte. He owed the bogus doctor that much for keeping the posse at bay.

"We're not a mile from the city limits," Jerrold said, pointing to a signpost with weathered lettering. "Why don't you jump off here and walk your horse into town? I'll be ready for you before you know it."

"Much obliged for all you've done," Slocum said. Jerrold fixed him with a gimlet stare, then nodded briskly and got his wagon moving toward Sentinel Butte. Slocum considered heading south, then put the idea from his mind. He did owe Josiah Jerrold. The walk into town gave him time to think about what he wanted to do. If the federal marshal in Fargo was all riled up, getting out of the territory was the smartest thing he could do. While riding on into Montana was appealing, that was likely the way most out-laws rode when leaving North Dakota. Slocum wanted a change of scenery like the kind Rapid City or Scotts Bluff might afford him.

As he entered town, he heard Jerrold's booming voice and saw that the snake oil salesman had pulled his wagon into an empty lot across the street from the bank. He teth-ered his horse and got to the back of the crowd to eavesdrop on what the men were saying. It was about as Slocum had expected. They all thought Dr. Jerrold was a fake. Slocum heaved a sigh. This was where he paid his due.

"That stuff doesn't work," he bellowed. People in the crowd turned to see who had the nerve to interrupt Dr. Josiah Jerrold.

"What's that? What are you saying, good sir? Are you claiming that Dr. Josiah Jerrold's Miracle Ache and Pain Elixir will not do as I claim? Step closer, sir. Step up, I say!"

Slocum pushed his way through the crowd. As he had guessed, they were mostly miners. No cowboys in Sentinel Butte. That meant aches and pains from long hours in a mine, along with a nasty cough caused by dust and damp.

"How can anything do everything you claimed?" Slocum hadn't heard what Jerrold boasted on, so he had to be vague. On impulse he began coughing hard.

"What ails you, sir? That's a mighty nasty rattle you got in your chest."

"Been working in a mine," Slocum lied. "Dust got me all choked up."

"One snort. Just one quick pull, that's all I ask."

Slocum took the bottle, sloshing some out as he coughed. He knocked back a shot of the vile brew and gagged. He coughed and then knew he had to continue with the show.

"It burned my throat—and it burned out my lungs, too. I don't feel like coughing anymore," he said with what he hoped was some sincerity. To his ears he was lying like a rug.

"It's good for aches and pains and what ails you, too," Jerrold said. "One dollar, sir. One dollar to cure your lung congestion for good!"

Slocum pulled out a many-times folded dollar bill and handed it to Jerrold in exchange for the rest of the bottle. This time when he put it to his lips, he forced his tongue into the narrow neck to keep from having to swallow any of the poisonous elixir. He licked his lips and proclaimed, "My shoulders aren't hurting like they were, either. This medicine works!"

Slocum knew he had to make an exit and did. The crowd pressed forward, all eager now to give their hard-earned money to Josiah Jerrold. Fetching his horse, Slocum led it around the bank and waited in back. He would return the bottle to Jerrold when the crowds cleared. There wasn't any reason to keep such a wretched potion when Jerrold could sell it to someone willing to lie to himself about its curative powers.

The crowd disappeared faster than Slocum had thought it would. He walked around and saw Jerrold enter the wagon, the dark curtain swaying after his exit from the drop-down stage. Slocum hastily jumped up and joined the doctor behind the curtain, inside the dim wagon.

"Thought you'd want this back." Slocum held out the bottle.

"You don't want to keep it?" Jerrold laughed. "Here's

your money back, and pay for the couple days we were on trail."

Slocum took the money but saw how sparse the remaining coins were.

"Not too good a business?"

"The whole damn town's hiding away, or so it seems. I tried to talk to the doctor, but he shooed me off like I was a leper. That's not too unusual, but he had a passel of people waiting to see him. I figured with so many sick folks, my business would be better." Jerrold shook his bald head sadly. "You never can tell. I'll be moving on right away. No need to stay when I've sold as many bottles as I'm likely to."

"I'll ride on, too," Slocum said. "South."

"A good direction for you. Me, I have a yen to see Montana. Haven't been there in such a long time the law's forgotten me. Might be the people buying my potion have, too."

"Or they want to believe it actually works."

"Faith, Slocum, faith is what's necessary in these hard times. You have faith in yourself, and I have faith in the gullibility of anyone exiling himself to live in a godforsaken hole like Sentinel Butte."

"Some will hit it big in the silver mines," Slocum pointed out. More than once he had fallen prey to the lure of the silver siren. He had made a few dollars but never enough to buy himself a fancy house up on Russian Hill in San Francisco and spend his evenings playing cards at the Union Club all gussied up in a tuxedo and swilling French brandy rather than tarantula juice. His card playing was more likely to be done in a saloon or dive along the Embarcadero.

"Then introduce them to me. I'm sure they need what I have to offer even more than the poor sots buying a pint of my elixir."

"Good luck, Doctor," Slocum said, thrusting out his hand. Jerrold shook.

"Sorry to part company, but it's for the best. I'm not sure what I'd tell that posse if they stopped me again."

"You'll never be at a loss for words," Slocum said.

"From your lips to God's good ear." Jerrold laughed, then said, "I'll be moving on soon since this town seems to be bordering on becoming a ghost town. From the number of buildings, I'd have thought there were a thousand people here. I hardly had twenty in the crowd."

"About that," Slocum said. Jerrold muttered something and turned away. Slocum considered riding with the doctor for another few days, then decided it was time to trust that Jerrold's liniment had worked on his mare's leg. Slocum returned to where he had left his horse and checked the leg. The mare didn't even shy away as he ran his fingers up and down the strained ligaments.

He patted the horse's neck, then mounted and let the horse find its own gait out of town. Slocum kept an eye peeled for the local marshal but saw only a few people. From the way everyone peered out at him, he might have been riding with Quantrill's Raiders again, ready to hurrah a Yankee town. The streets were deserted for this time of day, but he thought everyone might be hard at work in the silver mines in the steep hills surrounding the town. He was getting back into mountainous terrain, a relief after the utter flatness of the Dakota plains.

With the afternoon sun riding on his right shoulder, he headed south until he found an old road. Since it was easier following the winding road than cutting across the rocky terrain, he let his horse walk along it. As he fell into the rhythm of riding, Slocum dozed. His thoughts wandered and he wondered what it would be like if he came across the wagon train of the religious folks with the curious, foot-loose young boy. Settling down with a family would take a burden off his shoulders. Having a woman to depend on and to care for would be a major change to his life.

He jerked alert when he heard braying mules from

ahead. He had been half-dreaming about the settlers and must have somehow overtaken them. Slocum held his horse down to a walk, not wanting to strain the leg as he reached an abrupt slope where the road curled down the side of the steep hill. At the bottom of the hill, just starting up the winding road, came a wagon pulled by four mules. From this distance, the mules looked too small to drag such a load across the prairie, much less uphill.

His appraisal proved right when the mules balked and refused to budge when they hit the first incline.

"Get moving, you lop-eared monsters!" A woman stood and tried to crack a whip. She only lashed one mule on its rump rather than cracking the whip above the heads of the lead team. The mule protested and strained to get away— only it tried to run to the side. The harness hadn't been fastened properly, and the mule almost escaped.

Slocum put his heels to his mare's flanks to get down the hill as fast as possible. Slipping and sliding on the loose stones in the road threatened to send him and the horse on a catastrophic fall, but Slocum saw danger mounting second by second. The woman wasn't used to handling that many animals and might lose not only the one mule but her entire team.

"Drop the whip. Stop using it!" Slocum shouted.

She looked up, wild-eyed. Her hair fluttered behind her in the evening wind like a black banner, and even from this distance Slocum saw the intense blue eyes filled with fear. For a moment, she hung on the knife's edge of obeying him and using the whip to keep the wagon moving. Her decision didn't please Slocum any. She dropped the whip and grabbed a shotgun. By the time he brought his horse to a halt beside her team, she had the scattergun trained on him.

"I'll blow you to hell and gone!" she cried.

"You need help with your mules or not? If you do, put that down. You're going to hurt yourself and the mules."

He saw the mule in the second yoke braying noisily and

kicking out to free itself. The harness had tangled, and it slowly strangled itself.

"You can help?"

Slocum jumped to the ground and drew his knife. She gasped and raised the shotgun to train on him again, but he was moving fast to avoid the stomping mule's hooves. Slocum grabbed the harness and sawed through it, freeing the mule. It tried to run, but he hung onto what remained of the harness until the stubborn animal quieted.

"Get it hooked back," the woman said. "Do it right now or I swear, I'll fire!" She waved the shotgun around wildly. If she fired, it would not only knock her backward onto her pert ass, the buckshot would spray out in unknown directions. The mules would likely catch the bulk of the shot.

"I cut the harness to keep it from strangling itself. I need to fasten it back," Slocum said, knowing there was no way he could do this without mending the harness. She obviously hadn't any idea what had to be done.

"Please, please help me," she said, sinking to the hard driver's seat behind her. The shotgun sagged and pointed away. "I need help. I have to get into town as soon as possible."

"I got the idea you were in a powerful hurry," Slocum said. He studied the situation and worked out a way of attaching the mule to its partner. It would be pulling, letting the others do all the work, but this was better than losing the errant mule altogether.

"Is . . . is the mule back in harness?"

Slocum stepped closer. The sunset dropped golden rays onto the woman's face, revealing her real beauty. Her midnight dark hair was tangled like a bird's nest, but her handsome face was tanned and regular. Eyes bluer than the sky implored him for help. Her breasts rose and fell under her gingham dress bodice as she gasped and tried not to break down crying.

"The mule's hitched up again, but they're not strong

enough to get this heavy wagon up the slope. Even if you didn't have any cargo in it, they couldn't haul it up. You'd need at least four more, or a couple oxen."

"I . . . The wagon's not loaded. There wasn't time. I had to leave. I have to get to Sentinel Butte now!"

"You've got a half dozen miles once you get to the top of this hill. I'd offer to hitch my horse in to help your team but she's got a gimpy leg."

"You've done as much as you can. Thank you. I have to go." She pushed the shotgun aside and reached for the whip.

Four quick steps brought Slocum to her side. As she reared back to use the whip, he caught her wrist and held it in a steely grip.

Fear etched itself onto her face.

"You . . . you aren't—"

"I'm stopping you from hurting your team. I meant it when I said they can't pull this rig to the top of the hill."

"Let me go," she said hotly. "I don't care if I kill them. I don't care if I kill myself. I've got to get to town!"

"Why's that?"

The woman jerked free and dropped the whip as she faced him squarely.

"In the rear. Go look."

Slocum cautiously walked around and pulled back the canvas flap. She had been right about not driving a loaded wagon. All Slocum saw was a straw pallet and a man atop it, moaning softly and thrashing about weakly.

"That's my husband and he needs a doctor. Right now," she said. "If I don't get to town, Daniel's going to die."

From the man's pale aspect and sweaty face, Slocum doubted Daniel would last long enough to reach Sentinel Butte.

5

"What's wrong with him?" Slocum asked, although he had a suspicion. He had seen diphtheria before. He hesitated to get any closer to the man, moaning and thrashing about in the throes of his fever. The cough and the pallor were similar to what Slocum had seen during the war when an epidemic had wiped out close to a battalion from Georgia. He had avoided the worst of it because he had been ordered into the trees to watch for targets among the federal officer corps. Being a sniper had kept him alive then, and it had less to do with his marksmanship than it had to do with avoiding the infected men coughing on him.

"Whatever it is, I can't take care of him anymore," the woman said. "It was a terrible decision to make, but I have to get Daniel to Sentinel Butte where the doctor can look after him."

Slocum doubted the town doctor could do much. Even if the veterinarian and barber lent a hand, there wasn't much that could be done other than making the man comfortable and letting the disease run its course. More than half of his battalion had died and the rest had been left as weak as day-old kittens.

"Why was it such a decision? Can't you pay?"

"It's not that. My son. I had to leave him behind to look after the livestock on our farm."

Slocum nodded. He saw the difficulty the woman faced. It wasn't any of his business, not with the posse probably still sniffing around on his tracks, but he couldn't abandon her out here.

"I can drive your husband to town," Slocum said. "But not up this road. I'll have to find a road those mules of yours can climb."

"What do you mean?" The woman's eyes grew wide with fear. "You can't just go off and leave Daniel here. He has to get to town as quick as possible!"

"The only way I can see, if you don't want me to do some scouting, is to lash your husband to a mule. It can't climb the hill pulling the wagon, but with only a man, any of your animals can do the chore."

"But Daniel would . . ." Her voice trailed off as she realized the truth in what Slocum said. "Very well. Let me help you tie him down." She closed her eyes, sucked in a deep breath to steel herself, then opened her eyes again and thrust out her hand. "My name's Meghan Mallory and I am in your debt, sir."

Slocum shook her hand. It trembled in his grip. He introduced himself, then considered the best way of moving Daniel Mallory. When he began tearing away part of the wagon, Meghan protested.

"I'm making a travois. He's having trouble breathing."

"Well, yes, but—"

"Sling him belly-down over a mule's back and he'll suffocate within a hundred yards. This way he can keep on his back and try to breathe."

"You know what's wrong, don't you?"

Slocum told her his suspicions as he continued to pry loose planks from the wagon.

"Diphtheria? That's serious," Meghan said, her voice tiny and trapped.

"Not much that can be done, unless the doctor has some new medicine."

"You don't think so, do you?"

"I'm not a doctor," Slocum said, getting his material from the wagon. It took another fifteen minutes to securely fasten two planks to the sides of a mule and then drape a blanket between them. Slocum wrestled a feverish Daniel Mallory onto the blanket and then fastened him down. For a man of his height, he should have weighed twice what he did. The fever had worn him down to a nubbin.

"You can stay or ride a mule on back to your farm," Slocum said, looking up the hillside.

"I'm coming with you. I have to know."

Meghan refused to ride his horse and straddled a mule instead. They made their way up the steep road, Slocum aware of how the sick man's moans slowly died away. From occasional twitches, the man showed he was still alive, but Slocum didn't give him much longer.

Even with the lightened load for the mule, it took the better part of twenty minutes to reach the top of the hill. From there it was hours into Sentinel Butte. Traveling all night, keeping the pace slow to prevent jostling Daniel around too much, they finally reached the town just as the sun poked above the mesa that gave it its name.

"You've been so good, Mr. Slocum. If Daniel lives, it'll be because of you."

Slocum heard the despair in the woman's voice. They both knew the chance of her husband living more than a few hours was slim. Still, hope triumphed over what lay in front of her eyes.

"I'll see you to the doctor's office. It's down the street."

Slocum felt a cold knot forming in his gut the closer they got to the doctor's office. The sawbones had been busy. He had people in the street in front of his surgery, blankets pitched as tents to protect the patients. Slocum knew an epidemic when he saw one.

He dismounted and had started to go into the office when Meghan called out to him.

"Mr. Slocum? John?"

He turned and saw her kneeling beside the travois. Her lovely face was drawn and tears streaked her dusty cheeks. She didn't need to say anything more. Her husband hadn't lived long enough to have the doctor look at him, not that the doctor could have done more than tell her to keep Daniel's fever down with wet compresses.

"I'll see to it," Slocum said. He reversed course, took the mule's harness to tug it along with its dead load, and followed a frighteningly long line of citizens to the undertaker's parlor at the edge of town. It took some dickering when he finally got in, but Slocum arranged for immediate burial in a decent pine box. Searching all his pockets, he finally scraped together the exorbitant amount the undertaker demanded.

"I'm doing a land office business," the leathery, gaunt man said, rubbing his hands together as he took Slocum's money. He might have been a vulture sitting on a tree limb, only he didn't have to wait for something to die. Friends and relatives brought the dead to him.

"See that he's in the ground right away."

"The fever?"

Slocum only nodded.

"Like the rest. The doc's losing four or five a day."

"Put a decent marker on the grave. Daniel Mallory."

"It might take a while, but it'll be done. You have my word on that."

"I'll be back to check," Slocum said. The avarice disappeared from the undertaker's face, replaced by a sudden fear. His head bobbed up and down, giving his nose the aspect of a pecking beak. Slocum left, cutting the travois loose and leading the now unburdened mule back to where Meghan sat, staring at nothing in particular.

"It's taken care of," Slocum said. "You'll be able to get

the preacher to say some words, but it might be tomorrow before the grave's dug."

"There are so many," Meghan said. "I have to get back to the farm," she said suddenly. She stood, took the reins from Slocum, and tugged to get the mule moving to where the mule she had ridden stood patiently.

"You're not even going to see your husband buried?"

"I . . . My son. I have to think about Frank now. There's nothing more I can do for my husband. When things settle down, I can come back and pay my respects." She looked at him with pain and imploring in her teary eyes.

"I'll ride with you."

"I won't need the wagon returned. I can make it by myself." Her words said one thing but her expression said another.

"One direction is as good as another for me," Slocum said, "and I'd already chosen the one that crossed your path." He didn't need her words of thanks. The relief she felt was obvious in the way she rode on the mule.

They passed the wagon at the base of the hill and kept riding. Meghan never slowed, nor did she ask for Slocum to help hitch the team. Two mules had been left behind. Slocum caught up their harnesses and led them behind his horse. There was no call to abandon perfectly good animals because she was sorrow-wracked and not thinking straight.

They came to a double-rutted dirt path that led to a small farmhouse just as night fell. Slocum ached all over and needed some of Dr. Jerrold's elixir to quell the pain, but he didn't fish it out of his pocket. It wouldn't be right drinking what was low-grade whiskey just now. When he moved on and left Meghan with her son, then he would take a sip.

"Frank!" Meghan urged her mule on, but the animal was tired and wouldn't take one step faster than it wanted. She kicked her leg over, giving Slocum a look at a mighty fine naked limb. He felt a little guilty at wondering what the rest of her looked like naked, considering she had just lost her husband and all, but the guilt passed fast when he saw her throw open the front door and call for her son.

There wasn't an answer. Slocum led the mules to a small shed some distance from the house. He saw that the chickens hadn't been fed, and in a pen just beyond were three milk cows, all lowing in pain. They needed milking, if the bloated udders were any indication. The coldness Slocum had felt in town returned.

He hurried back to the farmhouse and looked in the front door. Meghan knelt beside a boy of twelve or so, stretched out on a couch. He moaned just the way his pa had—and he looked a world worse than the dead man. There was no color at all to his sweat-beaded face, though he might have seemed paler than he should because his hair matched his mother's in midnight intensity.

"He's got it, too," she said in a choked voice. "First Daniel, now my son. No, it's not fair!"

"Never is," Slocum said. "Fetch some water and clean rags. He has to be kept cool to prevent the fever from eating him up."

"You don't have to do this, Mr. Slocum. I can take care of him. You might catch it—the diphtheria."

"You keep cloth in the kitchen?" Slocum ignored her, went into the tiny kitchen, and rummaged about until he found a few dish towels. He saw that Daniel had built a small alcove off the kitchen for the pump. It took a bit of work, but Slocum filled a bucket with icy water from the well and carried it all back to the sitting room.

"Keep the cloths soaked and his forehead as cold as you can," Slocum said. He went to the door.

"John, wait. Thank you. If you ever come this way again, I'll leave the light out for you."

"The light might be useful right now," he said. "You've got cows to milk and chickens to feed. Any other livestock to tend?"

Meghan started to say something, clamped her mouth

shut, then smiled just a little as she shook her head. Slocum left to do the chores.

As he worked, he wondered how long he should stay. He had seen his share of fever victims, and Frank looked worse than most of them that died. Still, youth stood him in good stead. Boys were tougher than their slight features showed. Slocum had seen that during the war. When men who looked like bears flagged and dropped by the wayside, the scrawny youngsters kept marching and fighting on pluck alone.

He scattered grain for the famished chickens, having to kick a few of the more aggressive ones who decided to attack him. His boots kept the sharp pecks from hurting much. When he finished, he found a milking stool and a pail and set to work with the cows. They were temperamental, and all three tried to kick him until they got some relief from him draining their udders. He hated to waste the milk, but he poured out two buckets' worth since there was no way of keeping it.

As he carried the one full bucket back to the farmhouse, he wondered how long the boy had been sick. Judging from the lack of chores getting done, he might have been close to as sick as his pa when Meghan headed for Sentinel Butte in the wagon. Frank might have hidden it out of worry for his father or it might have hit him fast. Whatever the course of the disease, the farm hadn't seen any tending in a day and a half or longer.

At the door Slocum stopped and looked in. Meghan sat on a stool beside her son, hands folded in her lap. Slocum had seen her expression before. It was one of utter resignation. She realized it was only a matter of time before she lost her son, just as she had already lost her husband.

"He's looking a mite better," Slocum said, trying to bolster her spirits. The desolate look she gave him told him there was no need for such lies. She was tough enough to face the truth.

"There's a shovel in the shed. It's only a matter of time. If you don't want to dig the grave, I can understand and will do it when the time comes." She looked down at her son's unmoving form. His tortured, rattling breath moved his chest up and down the barest amount.

"Where do you want me to put it?"

"There's a tree twenty yards or so to the north. Frank liked to climb in the tree and swing off the limbs. I always told him to be careful, that he'd get hurt, but his father laughed at me and said he was only doing what boys do. That'd be a real good place."

Slocum took the milk into the kitchen and put the pail into a larger wash pan, which he filled with the icy water from the pump. It wasn't much but would keep the milk a tad longer. He silently went about the chore of digging the grave under the tree. It took longer than it ought to because he was in no hurry. He didn't feel like rushing things, even though he didn't have any doubt the grave would be needed soon enough.

When he had dug down far enough to keep the coyotes from sniffing it out and digging up the body when it was interred, he looked up into the sturdy oak and smiled. He had climbed trees like a monkey when he was a kid. He and Robert would dare each other to see how far up they could climb, and he had always won because he had been smaller and skinnier. When the weak limbs would sway and refuse to support his brother, Slocum always managed to get a few feet higher. That had been one of the few things he had ever bested Robert doing.

On impulse, Slocum began climbing. It was harder than when he was a child, but the effort not only brought back fond memories, it stole away thoughts of the death—deaths—of the past couple days. From limb to limb he climbed until he reached a spot where his adult weight was almost too much for the new limbs and shoots.

He clung to the trunk and looked out over the night-shrouded land. It was part prairie, part rocky foothills here. Daniel Mallory had planted several dozen acres and had a good crop on the way. Harvesting that much would have kept his family in food for the entire winter and still yielded seed corn for the next year. Everything had gone right for Daniel. Good land, good crops, a son, a lovely wife—and he had ended up worm food. It didn't seem right.

But then, Slocum had never found much that was fair or made sense.

Swaying a little as the wind kicked up a humid breeze, he was considering climbing down when he saw a lance of needle-thin light to the west. A second later came the sharp crack of a rifle. More muzzle flashes came, followed swiftly by the reports. Then a bonfire grew until the flames were searing the very clouds. Slocum watched and heard men shouting and laughing.

When the sound of horses approached from that direction, Slocum skinned down the tree and ran to the farmhouse. Trouble was coming at a gallop.

6

"You have a rifle or another scattergun?" Slocum called as he barreled through the front door. He remembered that she had left her shotgun with the wagon back at the base of the hill on the way into Sentinel Butte. Meghan looked up in surprise. "Do you?"

"Why, of course. A rifle. Daniel kept it over there." Even as she pointed, Slocum fetched the rifle and found a single box of cartridges with it. He hastily loaded it and handed it to her.

"You know how to use it? You're going to need to."

"What's wrong, John?" She looked down at her son and then back at Slocum. Her bright blue eyes locked with Slocum's green ones and read the danger. Her expression subtly altered.

If she had been frightened, Slocum would have had to deal with that. He saw a steel resolve settle on her. She would fight for her son to her last breath, no matter the challenge. With her husband dead, her son was all she had left in the world.

"Who lives in the house to the west?"

"The Parkmans. An older couple. All their children died, the youngest just the last winter from frostbite. Why?"

"I saw flashes from rifles and then a huge fire lit up the night."

"Their house caught fire?"

"I think they were murdered and their house was torched," Slocum said.

"But why? Who'd do that?"

"The epidemic must have spread farther and faster than anyone could figure," Slocum said. "Whenever this happens, bands of men go looting and murdering just for the hell of it."

"But Joanna and Peter," she said. "They're dead?"

"Most likely, and we will be, too, unless we're ready."

"I can fire a rifle. I'm not a good shot, but I bagged a rabbit or two for dinner when Daniel was working in the fields."

"We're not going to defend the house," Slocum said. "If they're willing to burn us out, there's no way to stop them. We've got to get Frank onto that travois and get out of here before the sons of bitches show up. How far was the Parkman house?"

"Two miles, maybe more but not much more," Meghan said.

"They won't gallop the whole way. They'll take their time, bragging about how brave they are killing unarmed men and women." Slocum stopped there. It was likely the outlaws had done more than just shoot Joanna Parkman. Unless she was lucky, she wouldn't have been shot until after they'd had their way with her.

Slocum scooped up Frank and carried him out the front door. The boy was feather light, but he seemed cooler than before. The compresses had brought down his fever, if not broken it. Getting jostled around caused the boy to moan. Slocum hoped he wouldn't give them away, because they'd have to hide. It wasn't possible that they could outrun the owlhoots coming this way.

"I've got a few things." Meghan swallowed hard. Slocum

saw a photograph of her and Daniel poking out the top of the carpetbag she had hastily packed.

"Any food?"

"I'll get it. Or do you need help putting Frank on the travois?"

"I can do it all right," Slocum said. He brought two mules around as well as his mare. The horse turned one huge brown eye accusingly on him. She had expected to be fed and get some rest before traveling again. Slocum patted the mare's neck, then slung the travois and lashed Frank down so he wouldn't bounce off. By the time he had finished, Meghan rushed from the house with a gunnysack of food and her carpetbag. She wasted no time slinging them on the mule and climbing up. She looked down at Slocum.

"Well? What are you waiting for? Let's go."

Slocum admired her spunk. He swung into the saddle and led the mule dragging the travois away, worrying about the twin ruts the poles left in the dirt. It was dark and lacked three or four hours until sunup. Slocum hoped the looters wouldn't notice their tracks. If they found the farmhouse deserted, robbing it and then setting fire to it might sate their bloodlust.

It might, but he didn't believe it. When men went crazy like this, murder and rape were all they sought. While they stole what they could, they only wanted an excuse to become animals. Worse.

They rode back in the direction of Sentinel Butte for a few minutes, but Slocum heard the owlhoots beginning to gallop down on the farmhouse. He and Meghan might be far enough away, but he didn't dare risk it.

"Keep going," he told her. "Get your boy to town."

"John, what are you going to do?"

He looked over his shoulder. The muzzle flash and report came together now. The raiders had reached the house and were only minutes behind.

"What I have to do. I'll meet you there." He saw that the

woman was torn between obeying because of her son and lending her support and rifle to whatever Slocum had in mind. Duty won out.

"Don't be long," she said.

Slocum stared at her. The woman's tone was different. Then she was gone, urging the mule she rode to hurry along. The mule dragging her son brayed loudly. Slocum swung his horse about to see if the noise had betrayed them.

It had.

He cursed under his breath, then did the only thing possible to give Meghan the head start she needed. He drew his Colt Navy and put his heels to his horse's flanks. He shot forward into the dark, galloping directly for the house. Two riders appeared suddenly in front of him, startled at his headlong attack. Their surprise let him fire twice to his left and three times to his right. He winged both men, sending one of them tumbling to the ground. The other's horse reared and forced its rider to struggle to stay seated.

"Jed, what's wrong?" The shout came from ahead of Slocum. He used his last bullet to force the man who must be the leader to duck. Then his pistol came up empty. Slocum slammed his six-shooter back into the holster and grabbed the rope coiled at his right knee. He swung the loop of rope and caught another man across the face.

All Slocum could do was sow discord. He galloped past, leaving the men behind. He heard the leader cursing his men and struggling to get them to pursue Slocum. Looping his rope over the saddle horn, Slocum worked to get his Winchester from its sheath. He fumbled, trying to keep his balance when his mare began dodging from side to side as lead sang after them. Wheeling about, Slocum lifted his rifle and hunted for targets.

"There he is. There's the—"

The man never finished his sentence. Slocum squeezed back on the trigger, felt the familiar thrust against his shoulder and knew his aim had been true. During the war he had served as a sniper for the CSA and had developed a sixth sense about the results of his marksmanship. More often than not he missed. Not this time.

"Yee-haw!" Slocum let out a cry of triumph and headed into the cornfield, hoping to decoy the outlaws after him. With any luck he could reach the far end of the row, turn, and pick off the raiders one by one, but it didn't work that way. Their leader had regained control. Slocum wondered if the man had military training or if those riding with him were deserters.

Whatever the truth, they didn't ride into his trap.

On the far side of the Mallory cornfield, Slocum trotted along until he reached a corner where he peered around at the looters. Rather than pursue, they had dismounted and were ransacking the Mallory house. He considered what to do. Without their horses, they would be sitting ducks. Or he could steal their horses and put an immediate end to their rampage.

Slocum could have done a lot of things, but he chose to slink off into the night and let the outlaws finish their despoiling. Without a good idea how many were in the band, he was at a severe disadvantage. Worse, he had only the ammo in his rifle's magazine. He had wounded a couple and perhaps killed another, but he still faced a small army.

Not liking the decision but knowing it was the right one, he rode away, angling off from the trail to Sentinel Butte. If the raiders came after him by tracking him, he wanted to lead them away from Meghan and her son. He doubted the town doctor could do anything for Frank Mallory, but the boy had seemed to be rallying. Slocum wasn't one to believe in miracles, but for Meghan's sake, he hoped for one now. She had already suffered too much with the loss of her husband.

After laying a false trail for almost an hour, Slocum decided there was no need to continue and cut back toward town. To keep riding in the proper direction, he checked the sky occasionally as the North Star poked through the thin, high clouds. He was bone tired but kept riding, knowing that Meghan would never flag on her way to Sentinel Butte. His horse was almost stumbling when he reached the outskirts hours later.

Two saloons were roaring with drunken fights in them. A gunshot rang out, but Slocum didn't even flinch. He was too intent on reaching the doctor's office. When he dismounted, he saw that the tent hospital had expanded—almost doubled. The epidemic was taking its toll on the town.

"You got call to see the doctor? You don't look sick." A man stepped out of the shadows to interpose himself between Slocum and the office door.

"I want to see if a friend got here with her son. Looked like the boy had diphtheria."

"That's what Dr. Wilson figured. Diphtheria."

"I won't have to bother him if you can tell me. Her name's Meghan Mallory and her son's called Frank."

"Too many showed up in just the last couple hours for anyone to keep track. Me, I got a sick wife and told the doc I'd help out."

Slocum understood. The man intercepted anyone who might take the doctor's attention away from his wife.

"Where're the newest patients?" From the haphazard way the tents had been strung up Slocum couldn't figure out where that might be.

"Can't say. Dr. Wilson comes out now and again to check the whole lot, but there ain't much he can do. You know about diphtheria? What can be done?"

"Saw it during the war. There wasn't anything the doctors could do, other than keep the afflicted cool and be sure they took water."

"You ought to be a doctor. That's what Wilson said."

Slocum heard loud voices that suddenly went quiet. This drew his attention more surely than if the boisterous behavior had continued. He reached for his six-shooter, then remembered he had run out of ammo. His rifle was securely in its saddle sheath some distance behind him.

"What . . . ?" started the man Slocum had been speaking to. This was all the farther he got before a meaty fist crashed into his face and knocked him backward. The man staggered, caught his heel, and fell heavily, hitting his head. He lay unmoving.

Slocum faced three wild-eyed and dangerous-looking men.

"Get the money. There's gotta be a lot of money. The sawbones has to be rakin' it all in."

"We shoulda robbed the bank," complained another of the men.

Slocum saw that the lawlessness had arrived in Sentinel Butte. The bands of looters out in the countryside were migrating to town, looking for easy targets.

The man with the knockout punch reared back to unleash another blow aimed at Slocum's face. Slocum moved faster than a striking rattler. He had his six-shooter out, cocked, and thrust into the man's face before the blow came.

"Let me shoot off your nose," Slocum said. "It's been a while and I need some entertainment."

The man backed off.

"We don't mean you no harm, mister. Hell, join us. This town's a plum waitin' to get picked. With so many sick, nobody's payin' attention to what's in the till. We kin steal it."

"I don't need money," Slocum said, walking forward and backing up the looter. "I want entertainment. I like killing sons of bitches like you."

From the corner of his eye, he saw the man's two partners going for their six-shooters. Since he was running a bluff with an empty pistol, he had to move fast. Slocum stepped up and swung the barrel of his Colt in a short arc that ended on the side of the man's head. The looter screeched in pain.

"You busted my ear!" His hand came away wet with blood that looked black in the starlight. Slocum didn't hesitate. He swung again, forcing the man to duck. As his victim turned, Slocum snared his six-gun. He had it out and cocked in his left hand in a flash.

Seeing their partner in trouble, both of the others opened fire. Slocum got off a shot that went wild. He wasn't dexterous enough to fire accurately with his left hand. Shoving his Colt back into its holster, he did a border shift, felt that the stolen gun was out of balance, and corrected. Two quick shots brought the nearest of the looters to his knees, clutching his belly. The remaining robber turned tail and ran. Slocum sighted in on him, but another shot rang out. The looter tumbled ass over teakettle and lay flat on his back groaning in pain.

A man came running up, clutching a rifle in his hands. He looked at the man he had just wounded, then used the rifle butt to good effect on the side of the outlaw's head.

He spun, barrel leveled and pointing at Slocum.

"Get those hands up. I'm the marshal."

"You got this all wrong, Marshal," Slocum said. "They wanted to rob Dr. Wilson." Slocum had found that the use of a name always gave a taste of truth to anything slipping over his tongue, especially when he was a stranger in town.

"Might be. You got anybody who can vouch for you?"

"I can," came a shrill voice. "Mr. Slocum helped me bring my son to the doctor. He's no crook." Meghan Mallory hurried from the doctor's office. In spite of the disheveled clothing and hair in wild disarray, she looked beautiful. "Put the gun down, Marshal. Please."

"Keep this one covered," Slocum corrected, grabbing the man he had buffaloed by the collar and spinning him around. "The three of them were going to rob the doctor."

"I seen three men robbing the telegraph office. Don't reckon that was the first place they stole from." The marshal came closer, patted down the man Slocum held, and pulled out a wad of greenbacks from a coat pocket. He shoved this under the man's nose and demanded, "Where'd a no-account like you get this much money?"

"Mine. Won it. Gamblin'."

"Like hell," the marshal said. "You're the kind who'd always draw to an inside straight. You're a damned loser, but now you've gone too far!" He pushed Slocum's hand off the robber's collar and grabbed it firmly. He shoved his rifle into the man's belly. "Come on along. I got a cell waitin' fer you and yer two buzzard-breath partners."

"Help me, please, I got shot in the belly." The man Slocum had shot writhed on the ground, clutching his midsection.

"Die, for all I care," the marshal said. He spat, then said, "I'll be back fer ya." He scooped up the man's gun from the dust and started toward the town jail with his prisoner.

"I didn't think you were coming, John." Meghan clung to his arm.

"How's Frank?"

"Not too good," she said. "Dr. Wilson is doing about what you suggested. Cool compresses to keep down the fever. Not much else can be done, except . . ."

"Except what?"

"I don't know. He wouldn't tell me. He gave Frank a spoonful of something that seemed to help, but the doctor wouldn't tell me what it was."

"Let's ask," Slocum said, giving the man he had wounded a quick look to make sure he wasn't faking. From the way the dark blood soaked his shirt and hands, it didn't seem likely. Left untended, the robber would die soon enough— and Slocum didn't much care. The doctor's time was better spent tending those sick with the diphtheria.

"Please, don't disturb him. He's pulled mighty thin, and I don't want him to stop giving Frank the medicine."

"I won't let that happen." Slocum tucked into his belt the six-gun he had taken from the robber. He had to be an imposing figure, one six-gun slung at his left hip and the other ready to draw from his belt. He was dusty from the trail and had blood spattered on his face from his foes.

He kicked open the door and went in. Dr. Wilson looked up guiltily and hid the bottle in his hand.

"What do you want? Get out of here! You're in the middle of an epidemic. These are sick people."

"What did you give Frank Mallory? Mrs. Mallory said it helped her son."

Slocum crossed the room and caught the doctor's wrist and twisted hard enough to see what was hidden. He had to laugh.

"You're knocking back Josiah Jerrold's snake oil? If you want, I'll get you a bottle of whiskey to keep you going."

"I'm not drinking this," Wilson snapped. The man's eyes were bloodshot and his hand shook, but Slocum heard the ring of truth in his words. "I ran out of medicine yesterday. When Charlie Lawson came in with the diphtheria eating him up, I gave him some of this since he had it in his pocket. I figured it would make his dying go a little easier."

Slocum looked intently at the doctor.

"What happened?"

"He got better." Wilson swallowed hard. His Adam's apple bobbed in a scrawny throat, looking like a bird swallowing a corncob. "Don't know why. Can't explain it, but he perked up. I started giving some to other patients, including the lady's boy. They all improved."

"Are they cured?"

"I don't know. I searched everyone for more of this devil's concoction but only found two bottles. This is all I have left." He held up the bottle for Slocum to see. Less than an inch of the potion remained. "It won't last long. Hell, I could use it all right away, and there are more patients coming in all the time."

"Dr. Josiah Jerrold's Magic Elixir works?" Slocum felt a little dizzy at the prospect. Jerrold was a fraud, an outright charlatan one step ahead of the law, and the potion was better used as a rust remover than a medicine. Or so Slocum had thought.

"I hate to say this, but it does," Dr. Wilson said. "Were you the one he used as a shill? I asked everyone I could. You answer to the description."

Slocum realized how serious Dr. Wilson was if he had asked everyone in the crowd who had gotten a bottle of the medicine.

"I rode into town with Jerrold," he admitted.

"I need more of the elixir," Wilson said. "As much as you can get. Jerrold left town right after his show. Bring him back with the medicine and you'll save half the population of Sentinel Butte."

Slocum looked across the room to the small, pale form of Frank Mallory lying on a blanket. "If I can save just one, that'd be fine with me."

Meghan gripped his arm with such intensity he felt the circulation dying, but he understood. Her son's life rested in his hands. If he could find Josiah Jerrold again.

7

"I've asked around and nobody knows what direction he went," Meghan said, looking drained. "I asked. I *asked*!"

Slocum took her in his arms when she began crying. He had tried to get a little sleep before getting on the trail. Dr. Wilson had staked him for grub and ammo to find Josiah Jerrold, but the doctor obviously worried Slocum would take the largesse and simply keep riding.

"You've done everything you could. I know ways of tracking him, even if the trail's gone cold."

"How?" Meghan asked. She kept her face buried in Slocum's shoulder. He felt her trembling like a fawn facing a mountain lion.

"He didn't retrace his route to Bismarck. There's no need to try selling his potion where he's already been. He mentioned wanting to press on into Montana. There's only the one road west that will take him there because he's in a broke-down wagon and has two horses better suited for a glue factory than to be a team. I can overtake him."

"You sound so sure, John. Are you always so sure of yourself?"

Slocum couldn't answer that. With her so close, the scent of her freshly washed hair in his nostrils, her warm, trembling body pressed into his, he knew what he wanted and this wasn't the time for it. Meghan had lost her husband days earlier and would lose her son if he didn't find Jerrold. Even if he had been inclined, Slocum knew time was a-wasting. He had to get on the trail.

"I've got something for you," he said.

Her face lit up and a tiny smile crept to her lips.

"What might that be? Something I'd like?"

"Something you can use," Slocum said, reaching into his pocket and pulling out the half-filled bottle of Josiah Jerrold's potion. "Don't let the others see it. Keep it for Frank."

"But you might need it. Dr. Wilson said it could prevent the sickness better than it could cure it."

"Take it. I can always get myself a bottle of whiskey that'll do the same thing for me."

She scoffed. "Whiskey's not medicine."

"It is if you have enough creaking bones," Slocum said, "from riding all day and half into the night."

"I'll get you a bottle, then. Two, if you can ride for twenty-four hours straight."

"No need," he said, laughing. "I already have a couple bottles. From the way Jerrold drank, I figure to use them to lure him back if he doesn't want to come."

"Are you going to tell him about the epidemic?"

Slocum didn't have an answer for that. Instead of facing this, he kissed her. It took them both by surprise. Slocum had acted impulsively and knew it was wrong, but from Meghan's startled, expectant expression he also knew it had not been unwelcome. Before the moment collapsed into awkwardness, he turned, stepped up into the saddle, and headed out of Sentinel Butte, going due west along the only road Josiah Jerrold could have taken.

He hadn't reached the edge of town when he looked back over his shoulder and saw Meghan watching him. She caught his eye, waved, and then disappeared into the doctor's office, clutching the half bottle of the potion he had given her.

The town was deserted, but he hadn't expected a crowd wishing him well. In its way, this was as secret a mission as any he had been given during the war. Dr. Wilson wasn't likely to raise the hopes of those with sick relatives or friends. If it took longer to get Josiah Jerrold back with his medicine, the survivors would blame the doctor—and Slocum—for not being faster. A certain number would die, even with the gut-twisting elixir, and there would be blame dished out no matter what. Wilson wanted to keep it to a minimum, and there was no way Slocum could fault him for that. It had to be bad enough watching friends and neighbors die. Being accused of letting it happen would only add to the sorrow.

In spite of the light sleep from the night before, Slocum found himself nodding off as he rode. His head sagged forward and he fell into the hypnotic rhythm of the walking horse. He snapped awake every mile or two and kicked the horse to a quicker gait, but when he dozed, the horse slowed.

Slocum didn't mind that too much. He had to be rested to do some real tracking when he got farther down the trail, and his horse had to be fresh, too.

All day he rode, eating in the saddle and taking short breaks only to water his mare and let her crop some grass. He pushed steadily, galloping, then dropping to a walk and picking up the gait to a trot and back to a walk. The ever-changing pace devoured distance without killing his horse.

By sunrise the next day Slocum found himself at a crossroads. One branch went toward a small town whose name had been weathered off the signpost entirely. There might have been a B in the name and possibly it was named Something-or-other City. The second road twisted toward the range of low mountains directly north. Slocum knew Jerrold had to sell his potion in towns, but something about the road into the hills drew him. Although it could be a waste of time and might set him back a half day, he turned into the hilly country and let his horse set its own pace.

When he saw the deep ruts in mud near a stream, he knew his hour-long sojourn had not been in vain. He rested his mare as he studied the tracks. When he found a discarded label for Dr. Josiah Jerrold's Revitalizing Tonic, he knew he was on the right track. Jerrold had printed a new label. The ink was still damp, and his thumb came away green when he touched it. Slocum didn't know how fast ink dried, but he knew he had to be close to the snake oil salesman.

Anxious to find Jerrold but cautious about tiring his horse overmuch, Slocum walked for another hour before he came to a mountain glade with a gentle stream running down from the higher elevation. Parked next to the stream was Jerrold's medicine wagon. Of the doctor he saw nothing. Approaching warily, Slocum got within a few yards of the wagon before the dark curtain hiding the interior was yanked back. Josiah Jerrold poked his head out, squinted, then put on glasses and peered at Slocum.

"What the hell are you doing here, boy? I thought you were dodging the posse by going south."

"I ran into a bigger problem than a federal marshal."

"Now, whatever could that be? Come on over and tell me. I love a good tall tale."

"Not good and not a story," Slocum said. He quickly detailed all that had happened. Jerrold didn't interrupt, and even after Slocum had finished, the doctor said nothing. He only shook his head in disbelief.

"Can you help? How much of the elixir have you made up?" Slocum pulled out the freshly printed label he had found and handed it to Jerrold.

The peddler looked at it and then up at Slocum. A slow grin came to his face.

"You didn't strike me as the charitable sort. Why are you

getting involved? And what's that farmer's lovely widow's name?"

Slocum cursed Jerrold for being too astute an observer of human nature, but it was his profession. He sold worthless patent medicine and had to find the right arguments to make the buyer believe it was God's own elixir. Of course he would see straight through to the heart of the matter.

"I've got a couple bottles of whiskey for you to use as base, in case you ran out of alcohol."

"How'd you happen to find me? It's more reasonable to think I went on to whatever that city was to sell more of my belly burner."

"Can't say. A hunch."

"Does your hunch tell you also that the reason I headed for mountains where herbs grow was to replenish my stock? I've run out of damned near everything that went into the last batch—the potion I sold in Sentinel Butte."

"Let's get to collecting. Tell me what you're looking for."

"Not so fast, son. That formula was a little bit fudged, if you take my meaning."

"I don't. You mean to say you don't know what you put into it?" Slocum held back rage and a feeling of helplessness.

"Not exactly. Now, don't get all riled, but I stole that recipe from a Sioux medicine man. He claimed it had all kinds of curative powers. In Bismarck I used that as a selling point. Indian medicine, secret known only to a shaman, that kind of a pitch. But I couldn't find all the roots and leaves, so I improvised to give it about the same taste."

"What did you put in?"

Jerrold looked thoughtful and finally said, "You see that lacy-leafed plant yonder? That's likely to be what makes Dr. Josiah Jerrold's Curious Curative so effective. I found a patch and picked it all, using it in addition to the rest of the herbs and liquor."

"How much would you need to whip up a batch for an entire town?"

"Can't say, but more'n's growing there. A lot more."

Slocum went to the low-growing plant and snapped off a leaf and rubbed it between his fingers, then took a deep sniff. The aroma made him woozy.

"See? Powerful medicine," said Jerrold. "Don't rightly know what it is since I'd never seen it before, but that ignorance never stopped me from making mighty fine medicine."

"I'll get to collecting as much as I can find," Slocum said. He took a deep breath to clear his head, and the dizziness passed. The lacy-leafed plant between his fingers was as strong as anything he'd ever seen this side of locoweed.

"Don't be gone too long," Jerrold warned. He held up a bottle of the whiskey Slocum had brought. "I might be tempted to sample this. Just a nip or two . . . or three."

"I won't be too long. Plants grow in rows, or so it seems. Looks as if this grows in a straight line going into the forest." Slocum took a burlap sack and began collecting, careful to avoid inhaling the freshly crushed plant.

He worked diligently for twenty minutes and was surprised when he came upon a barbed wire fence. The plant grew under the wire and extended across another meadow in a wide swath. He climbed the fence and continued picking the plant. The bullet ripping past his ear, tearing a hole in his hat brim, took him entirely by surprise.

He dropped the bag, fell facedown to the ground, rolled and got his six-shooter out, and recovered his balance. Half-sitting, he looked to see where the bushwhacker hid. He didn't have to hunt. Two men stalked out of a stand of trees, rifles aimed in Slocum's direction.

"Whoa, there's no need to take a potshot at me. All I was doing—"

"No need to lie. Just get your sorry ass off my property."

"I need the—" Slocum hefted his six-shooter and aimed when both men raised their rifles to their shoulders. "I don't want a shoot-out with you. I only want the plant."

"I don't want to bury your worthless corpse, either, and I surely don't want to leave it rottin' so's it'll poison a coyote. Get off my land. Didn't you see the fence?"

Slocum cautiously came to his feet, never letting his six-shooter stray from the older man doing the talking. The younger man with him looked nervous. Judging from the similarity in their noses, cheeks, and jaw structure, he spoke with the father while the son wasn't sure he wanted to cut down a trespasser at all.

This let Slocum concentrate on the older man.

"This is medicine. There's an epidemic raging over Sentinel Butte way and—"

"I know all about that. That's why you're not gonna stay on my property one second longer. I don't want you bringing the plague in to kill me and my family. I been through that once before back in Ohio. I came out here to get away from all the sickness, and you're not givin' it to me or mine!"

Slocum saw the man's finger tightening on the trigger.

He took a chance and lowered his Colt.

"I'm going. Might be I can buy some of this plant from you?" He pointed to the lacy-leafed plants.

"I'll count to ten and open fire. One."

Slocum picked up his burlap sack and got over the fence before the rancher reached eight. There was no point antagonizing him. Slocum trooped back to Josiah Jerrold's wagon and gave the doctor what he had collected.

"Is this enough?"

"For a bottle, maybe two," Jerrold decided, hefting the bag and peering inside. "This all you found?"

Slocum sucked on his teeth a moment and shook his head.

"I can get a lot more," he said, remembering how the meadow had been carpeted with the plant. The only trouble he might have was sneaking back to get it with the rancher and his son so vigilant, but it had to be done.

"Before you get into more trouble," Jerrold said, "sit here, take a swig of this horrible whiskey you brought me, and tell me all about her."

"Her?"

"The filly that's got you galloping all over North Dakota looking for an old geezer like me so you can fetch her more of my nostrum. That's who."

Slocum was reluctant, but Jerrold coaxed out more of the story of the looters attacking the Mallory farmhouse and how Slocum had decoyed them away so Meghan could get her son to town safely.

"You've got the makings of a hero, Slocum. No, don't scoff. Not many men would risk their precious hides the way you did. Not many men would sneak back onto another man's land to steal medicinal plants, either." Jerrold took a long pull on the whiskey and handed the bottle to Slocum, who hesitated. "Go on, fortify yourself. I don't need but a little alcohol to make a tincture." Jerrold laughed and took another drink. "Listen to me and the way I talk. You'd think I had all the fancy education I claimed."

"Don't you?" Slocum asked, not knowing why. From the way Jerrold reacted, he knew he had struck a nerve.

"No." The denial was flat and harsh, and Slocum thought it was a bald-faced lie.

"I'd better take another sack and begin harvesting," Slocum said, seeing he had touched a sore spot in the old man's soul. He took two, tucked them under his gunbelt, and set off through the twilight, retracing his earlier path. The odor from the plants he had plucked filled the air and made him a tad giddy, but he pushed on and quickly came to the barbed wire fence. He climbed it, paused, and listened hard for any sound in the gathering evening. All he heard was insects buzzing about and the faint whisper of wind trying to rustle leaves in the post oaks and cottonwoods.

He found the edge of the patch where he had been shot at

and began picking with quick, sure movements. It took him a considerable time to work across the field. After filling one burlap bag, he began on the second. How much of the medicine Jerrold could concoct from this amount of leaves was something Slocum would have to find out. If necessary, he could hunt for more while Jerrold returned to Sentinel Butte with what elixir he had whipped up.

Slocum angled through the meadow, going toward a stand of oak at the far side. From what he could tell, the plants he sought grew about everywhere. He picked faster.

When he found a particularly thick clump, he dropped to his knees, heaved a fallen log away, and began pulling with both hands and stuffing the leaves into his bulging second bag.

He heard the crunch of a footstep behind him an instant too late. He swung about, hand going to his Colt Navy just as the rifle butt smashed down into his forehead.

8

Sunlight burned his face. Slocum blinked hard and tried to focus, but he stared directly into the rising sun. He turned his head and tried to figure out why he couldn't move. Slowly working through the tiny facts brought him to a gut-wrenching realization that he was securely tied to a tree. As his vision cleared and he looked around, squinting hard against the sun, he saw that his initial guess was partly wrong.

He was tied not to a tree but to a thick post set in the middle of a field. Twisting and turning convinced him someone had done a damned good job of binding his wrists behind him, the post holding him upright. He craned his neck around and saw that the post extended three feet above his head. For a moment the wild thought of somehow inching his way up the post and getting free gave him hope. All hope vanished, however, when he saw this was impossible.

Slocum rocked back and forth, slamming hard against the post to loosen it from the ground. He might as well have been trying to move an ancient oak tree.

"Ain't gonna do you no good," came a tremulous voice. Slocum worked around and got the sun out of his eyes to see the rancher's son standing with his rifle leveled.

"Afraid I'll jump you?" Slocum saw the way the boy jumped.

"You stay back."

"I don't have much choice," Slocum said. "You the one who bushwhacked me? That was a cowardly thing to do."

"You hush your mouth," the young man said. He waved his rifle around. Slocum wasn't afraid of being shot, because the control of the rifle wasn't there. He was afraid of what the young man's father might do. The rancher had been adamant about trespassers. Being trussed up as he was showed he was in a world of trouble.

"Let me go and you won't see me again."

"I can't get near you or I'll git sick and die."

"What?" It took Slocum a few seconds to understand. "You think I've got diphtheria?"

"I'm not gonna risk it. Folks in these parts have been dyin' and we heard 'bout Sentinel Butte. Everyone's dead there. Every last damned soul!"

"Don't go cussin', Aaron."

Slocum scooted around another half turn and saw the rancher stomping toward them. The man carried a sack with him that clanked as he walked. He dropped the sack and went to stand beside his son.

"I'm sorry, Pa."

"You ought to be. You know what cussin' does to your soul. Turns it blacker than an old iron kettle."

"Not as much as bushwhacking me and tying me up," Slocum said. He rubbed the ropes binding his wrist against the rough post, but wearing down the strands would take the rest of the day. His hands had already turned numb from lack of circulation. Without being too obvious, Slocum dug in his heels and arched his back, pressing into the post as hard as he could from a new direction. He hoped he could loosen it enough to pull it out of the ground and get free. It didn't budge, no matter how he rocked and pushed.

"You won't have to worry long 'bout the sun in your eyes," the rancher said.

"I'll be out of your hair as soon as you get the ropes off me," Slocum promised. "I would like to keep the leaves I collected. They might not cure the diphtheria, but they ease the symptoms."

"Won't matter none to you. We got to protect our own, and you admit you were in Sentinel Butte."

"I was, but—"

"You're carryin' the plague, then. Never heard of anyone passin' through that didn't have it. My neighbors all around are comin' down sick because of that hellhole. I got to protect my own. I got to," the rancher said, as if convincing himself of some ultimate truth.

Slocum caught his breath when he saw the rancher take a bottle of kerosene from the sack. The man pulled the cork and sloshed the volatile fluid around, then splashed it all over Slocum.

"Fire. I need fire to burn away the source of infection. You got a lucifer, Aaron?"

"Pa, I don't know about this."

"Listen to your boy," Slocum said. His heart threatened to explode as the rancher started hunting for a match. "You don't want the law coming here. The sheriff will hunt you down. He'll come from Sentinel Butte and bring the plague with him."

The rancher looked at Slocum with fire in his eyes. Then the fire appeared between his fingers as he dragged a lucifer across his thigh. The flame danced in the humid breeze fitfully blowing across the meadow.

"I don't want to do this, but you shouldn't have tried to infect me and mine. Fire's the only way to cleanse the plague." He stepped forward. Slocum fixed on the match burning in the rancher's hand.

The thunder of hooves distracted the rancher for a moment, allowing Slocum to kick out. The toe of his boot caught the man's wrist, forcing him to drop the lucifer. From somewhere Slocum gathered strength he had never known he possessed and heaved. The post finally came free. Slocum toppled backward and landed hard.

"Kill him, Aaron. Shoot the son of a bitch!"

"Pa, you shouldn't cuss."

"Don't tell me what to do, you little turd!"

The two fought over Aaron's rifle, giving Slocum precious seconds to worm his way up the post and get free. His hands were still tied behind his back, but he rolled over and got his knees under him. As he looked up, he saw the source of the noise that had distracted the rancher. Dr. Jerrold clung to Slocum's horse as if he had never straddled a horse before. He galloped toward them, then began shouting and waving his left hand to further distract the father and son struggling over the rifle.

Slocum got to his feet as Josiah Jerrold reined back. The old man reached down and grabbed Slocum's collar and pulled him off his feet with surprising strength. Flopping belly-down over the mare's rump, Slocum almost bounced off as Jerrold wheeled around and retraced his path across the meadow.

The rancher finally wrested the rifle from his son and sent a couple bullets winging after them. His aim was off, and Jerrold reached the woods before the man got the range.

Once they were safely out of sight, Slocum slid off the horse, tried to land on his feet, and ended up falling on his butt. He sat on the leaf-strewn forest floor staring up at Josiah Jerrold.

"You ever ride a horse?"

"Not for years. There is a reason I drive a wagon." Jerrold stepped down and rubbed his behind. "I can use a pillow to ease the pain I feel in a certain part of my anatomy that is tortured unduly by being astride a saddle."

"You have hemorrhoids," Slocum said, "and your elixir doesn't do a damned thing for them."

"Something like that," Jerrold said. He pulled a penknife from his pocket and sawed at the ropes around Slocum's wrists.

The sudden release of pressure made Slocum wince. Circulation returned painfully, making his flesh feel as if some demon poked fiery needles into his wrists. He rubbed them until the pain receded.

"Thanks for pulling my fat out of the fire." Slocum sniffed and realized that was an exact description of what had happened. "How'd you happen to come just when I needed you?"

"When you didn't return, I followed your trail, saw your plight and tried to decide how best to rescue you since it was obvious you were not going to free yourself."

"Mighty fancy tracking."

"I have talents of which you are not aware," Josiah Jerrold said haughtily. Then he dropped the pose and asked, "Did you get the leaves?"

"I must have dropped the sacks where they bushwhacked me." For the first time Slocum realized he still wore his Colt. He touched the ebony handle in wonder. "They didn't even disarm me."

"Fear of diphtheria makes a man do crazy things," Jerrold said. "I overheard a little of what was said. The man's fear prevented him from ever touching you or anything you carried."

"That's luck," Slocum said, drawing the six-shooter and checking to be sure it hadn't been tampered with. It was fully loaded and ready for use.

"You going back for the leaves?" Josiah Jerrold stared at him appraisingly. "You're a bigger fool than I thought. Either that, or that filly's prettier than any widow woman has a right to be."

Slocum ignored the jibe and swung into the saddle. Medicinal plants or no, he had a score to settle. The rancher and his son had tried to burn him alive. The stink of kerosene on his clothing refused to go away, and wouldn't until he scrubbed his shirt and jeans good and proper. If they didn't want visitors, that was one thing, but they didn't have any call setting a man on fire.

When he reached the edge of the meadow where he had been staked out, Slocum hesitated. Neither the rancher nor his boy was in sight. All that remained as mute testimony to their intended crime was the uprooted post in the middle of the field. Slocum trotted directly for it, slowing only when he reached the spot where the fight had been. From the muddled tracks he guessed the rancher and his son had set off at an angle to where the plants grew. Their ranch house was probably in that direction.

He'd had enough fight for the day and wanted to peaceably gather his leaves—and yet he itched for a fight. The rancher was a sidewinder who deserved to have his head chopped off and left to wiggle until sundown. Slocum reached the spot where one of them—probably the rancher—had slugged him. Both sacks of leaves had been kicked aside. A quick dismount and he was ready to begin his harvesting again.

Both bags were stuffed as full as he could get them, and Slocum had started back for his horse, when he caught the glint of sunlight off a rifle barrel. He tied the bags together and tossed them over his mare's rump, fastening the sacks just behind his saddlebags. As if he were unaware of the sniper drawing a bead on him, Slocum walked around the horse, then grabbed for his rifle. It slipped free and came to his shoulder in one smooth movement.

He drew back on the trigger and sent leaden death sailing through the still afternoon air, but his innate sense told him he had only winged his would-be killer. From the bull-throated curses coming from the sniper's direction Slocum knew he had shot the rancher.

That was fine with him.

He levered another round into the chamber and started

walking directly for the place where the rancher hid. Another round tore past Slocum, but he paid it no heed. He had become a force of nature, not to be denied. The rancher panicked and bolted. That was the last thing he ever did. Slocum sighted in on the man's back and fired. This time his sense told him he had made a kill.

When he reached the body, he saw that the rancher had died instantly. The bullet had shattered his spine.

"You died too easy," Slocum said.

As he looked around, he heard distant noises approaching, as if a dozen men came to see what the gunfire was about. If this was a working ranch, the son might have called on the services of a half dozen or more cowboys. Slocum was still spitting mad, but he wasn't stupid. He didn't have the ammunition or the time to fight it out with a small army. Getting the plant leaves to Jerrold was more important than soothing his own ruffled feathers. Besides, the architect of his demise had died with a bullet in his back. The sight of the body made it possible to endure the smell of kerosene soaked into his shirt and jeans. Almost.

He glared at the rancher's body, spun, and returned quickly to his mare. He mounted and trotted off, disappearing into the woods as the rancher's son and four men came into view waving around rifles.

Slocum felt vindicated for what he had done. The rancher had deserved to die.

That chore finished, he had a more pressing one ahead of him. He reached Jerrold's encampment and found that the old peddler had hitched his team and waited impatiently.

"You have the leaves? Give them to me. All of them. You drive while I work. Try not to hit too many potholes. I want a fresh batch of the potion ready by the time we get back to Sentinel Butte."

Slocum didn't argue. He hitched his mare to the rear of the wagon, climbed into the driver's box, snapped the reins, and they rattled away, heading for town. With any luck, Jerrold's vile elixir would work miracles and Frank Mallory wouldn't die.

Slocum didn't believe in luck. He bellowed out a command and got the team pulling just a little faster.

9

Slocum tried to find the smoothest section of the road, but going back downhill toward the junction leading to Sentinel Butte challenged his skill as a driver at every turn. The only people using this road were probably those going to the ranch owned by the man Slocum had shot down. Killing him had been a pleasure, though Slocum wished he could have seen the man's face as he died.

If he had succeeded in murdering Slocum, dozens, if not hundreds, more would have died from the diphtheria.

"Be careful," came Jerrold's irritated command from the rear of the wagon. "This is a delicate part of the extracting. I'm boiling out the juices and distilling them down to use in the potion."

Slocum didn't bother answering. He steered carefully around the corner and onto the road to town. The going was easier now because the added traffic along the road had kicked out the larger rocks and left only hard-packed dirt behind.

It was easier driving, but Slocum found that his nerves were more on edge. He spotted movement off to the side of the road. As he turned, he caught sight of two men astride their horses doing all they could to avoid being seen. If that had been the posse after him, they would have boldly ridden up to find who was in the wagon. Running for cover the way these men did told Slocum they were up to no good.

The looters who had attacked the Mallory house might be long gone. Others wouldn't be. As men and women died, the veneer of civility cracked and exposed the real animal natures beneath. With the threat of retribution removed, it became easier for some men to steal and pillage. From all Slocum had seen, the town marshal in Sentinel Butte had his hands full and wasn't likely to poke his nose beyond the city limits.

Slocum had threatened the rancher and his son with a visit from the sheriff, but he had no idea where the county seat was—or even what county he drove through. If the diphtheria had spread, the law would be occupied with more serious matters than handfuls of looters. Keeping whole towns from getting burned to the ground mattered more than investigating an occasional farmhouse ablaze.

"Can you fasten down your bottles?" Slocum shouted back.

"You cannot be serious! I need my glassware more than ever at this point. What are you planning to do?" Josiah Jerrold stuck his head through the curtain dividing the wagon from the driver's bench.

"We got company. It's like being followed by a pack of wolves." Slocum jerked his thumb in the direction where he had seen the riders.

"Have you ever watched a pack of wolves go after a moose?" Jerrold asked unexpectedly.

"I suppose."

"Then you know what they do. The weakest of the pack line up on both sides of the moose and nip at its legs. Not a one of them could bring down such a magnificent beast."

"The moose runs," Slocum said, getting the picture. "The females and weaker males herd the moose until the leader can attack."

"By the time they've finished chasing and herding the moose, it is considerably weakened and less of a match for a strong wolf."

Slocum got the drift. He looked to the other side of the road and saw three riders there as well. Just like the moose in Jerrold's story, they were being herded. That meant an ambush awaited them ahead. He slowed the pace considerably, until they were moving along at hardly more than a walk.

"What do you intend to do, son?"

"Let you drive for a spell. Can you put your concocting on hold?"

"I can," Jerrold said. He vanished into the rear of the wagon. After a minute of glass clinking and a little bit of swearing on the peddler's part, he reemerged and dropped gingerly onto the hard seat beside Slocum. He silently took the reins, letting Slocum move along the exterior of the wagon and mount his horse dutifully trotting along behind. He unfastened the reins and dropped back, letting Jerrold spring the trap.

Slocum drew his rifle and watched either side of the road. The outliers had ridden ahead, confident of their planning.

He cut away from the road and found the tracks of three riders on the left side of the road. He spurred his horse to more speed and brought his rifle up to his shoulder, ready to fire. The instant he saw one of the outlaws laying in wait, he fired. His round went wide, but it shocked the other road agents so much they revealed their hiding places. They popped up like prairie dogs to see what was going on.

Slocum showed them.

He winged two and flushed another pair, sending them running for their horses. Having fired the rifle until his magazine came up empty, he drew his six-shooter and charged the remaining outlaw. The man tried to fight. Slocum took him to be the leader.

Then he was the dead leader. Three rounds from Slocum's six-gun tore through the man's chest. One might have hit his heart, but it hardly mattered. He sank to the ground like a marionette with its strings cut.

By the time Jerrold drove up, Slocum had finished searching the dead outlaws. The wounded ones had crept off into the woods, and the others were probably in another county, still riding as if the demons of hell nipped at their heels. And, for a brief instant, that had been true.

Slocum reloaded and called to Jerrold, "Keep driving. These galoots won't bother you anymore. I need to see what's on our back trail."

"You thinking there's more?"

"I know there are more. This isn't the same bunch that attacked the Mallory house."

"Don't do anything foolish," Jerrold said. "I might need someone to pick more of them leaves, and with my hemorrhoids the way they are . . ."

Slocum waved him on, grinning. He stepped up into the saddle and hurried back to see if the gunfire had attracted attention.

"Damn," he muttered when he saw the rancher's son riding along. The young man rode slowly, looking at the road as if he had to track Slocum this way. Slocum would have taken him out, but he had run out of ammo for his rifle and the distance was too great for a handgun. A dozen ways of dealing with the problem ran through his head, but there had been killing aplenty, and Slocum felt the need to reach Sentinel Butte without more. The youngster rode so slowly it would be hours before he reached town anyway.

By then Slocum would have seen the potion safely delivered to Dr. Wilson and have gotten an idea how Frank Mallory fared. He turned around and galloped away. A final look over his shoulder before a bend in the road robbed him of view showed the youngster still plodding along, occasionally switching his gaze to the opposite side of the road.

Slocum hoped that he never reached Sentinel Butte.

Within minutes Slocum had overtaken the medicine wagon.

"That was quick," Jerrold called. "Didn't hear any gunfire, either."

"No need." He didn't bother letting Jerrold know what the real problem was. If the rancher's boy thought on it for a moment, he'd have realized that the road didn't lead anywhere but into Sentinel Butte. He should have been riding faster. He had plenty of reason to gun Slocum down, but he was riding way too slow to ever overtake anyone.

This bothered Slocum.

"You got a look about you I don't like," Jerrold said. He pulled back on the reins and slowed his team. "What's eating you?"

"You should get on into town," Slocum said. "I have to find what's wrong with . . ."

"Who was following us? The rancher's kid?"

Slocum nodded. He thought back on how the youngster swayed form side to side. He wasn't tracking; he was barely hanging onto the saddle horn.

"Keep going. I'll catch up."

"What about the owlhoots out there raiding? I can't hold them off," Jerrold said.

"Won't take long. Either this will be over quick or—"

"Or you get yourself shot up." Jerrold snorted. "I'll keep rolling at a steady pace, but you need to think more about what's ahead than what's behind, son."

Slocum knew the snake oil peddler was right, and it didn't matter. He wheeled about and galloped back around the bend to where he had a view of the road. The rancher's son had stopped in the middle of the road and tottered about. As Slocum watched, the youngster fell out of the saddle and hit the ground hard enough to spook his horse.

Approaching slowly, Slocum watched to be sure he wasn't riding into a trap. The body on the ground hardly stirred. When Slocum saw that the youngster wasn't armed, that he had depended entirely on his rifle and that was in the saddle sheath of the horse that had run off, he stepped down and went to the boy's side.

He prodded the body with his toe and got a moan in response. Slocum bent over and put his hand on the exposed forehead. He pulled back when he felt how the boy was burning up with fever. His pa had worried about his family catching diphtheria. He had died without knowing his efforts had been in vain. His son was being eaten up alive by the disease.

Slocum looked around for the boy's horse, but the animal had headed for the tall grass. Tracking it would take too long. Slocum knelt, got his arms around the boy's hunched shoulders, and then heaved. He staggered back a step, then swung around and heaved the rancher's son belly-down over the mare's saddle. She protested even more when Slocum mounted.

"Come on. We don't have far to go," he assured the mare. He walked her slowly and still managed to overtake the medicine wagon before Jerrold reached the outskirts of Sentinel Butte.

"You're plumb outta your mind," Jerrold said, shaking his head when he saw who Slocum had rescued. "You could have left him to his own devices. His pa wanted to turn you into a bonfire and the boy didn't do much to stop him."

"He's got the diphtheria," Slocum said. "That's not his fault."

"If you think I can cure him with my elixir and that he'll thank you, you've got shit for brains."

"I'm not looking for him to love me," Slocum said. "I just don't want to have to kill him when he gets well."

"If he gets well," Jerrold amended. "I do declare, I've never seen anyone like you, Slocum. One minute you can kill a man and never bat an eye. The next you're risking your own life for someone who's not going to appreciate the effort, not one little bit. No, sir."

Slocum grinned crookedly and worked to pull the rancher's son out of the saddle and load him into the rear of the wagon. He rolled the youngster in a blanket to cushion some of the shocks from the rough road, then stepped back, having done all he could. He called to Jerrold and the man snapped the reins, getting back on the road to town.

They reached Sentinel Butte an hour later. The streets were deserted, and the only sounds Slocum heard were distant cows lowing and the wind blowing around the buildings.

He had seen ghost towns that looked livelier.

10

"I don't like this," Josiah Jerrold said in a low voice. "It's not natural, being so quiet."

"Keep driving," Slocum said. He caught motion from the corner of his eye. He slipped the leather thong off the hammer of his Colt Navy and turned slightly to better draw if the need arose.

It did. Fast.

A huge cry went up as a half dozen townspeople charged at them from a narrow alley between two buildings. Slocum drew and fired into the air above their heads. All but one of the crowd stopped. Slocum took more careful aim at the burly man lumbering forward, waving an axe handle above his head. The bullet nicked the man's leg and twisted him about. He righted himself and came on. Slocum's mare began crow hopping.

"Stop! I don't want to shoot you but I will!"

"Get out of our town. You're bringin' the plague with you!"

"They got a diseased son of a bitch in the wagon. I see him all thrashin' about!" Two others from the crowd circled and peered inside Jerrold's medicine wagon.

"Back," Slocum said. "Get back!" He fired when the

burly man did not obey. The first shot had left a shallow, bloody groove down his thigh. This slug caught the man squarely in the shoulder. It didn't affect him at all. He rushed on.

This time Slocum took even better aim and hit a knee-cap. The man lurched and then crashed forward onto his face, thrashing about in the dirt and screaming incoherently.

Slocum swung his six-shooter around and brought it to bear on the men trying to pull the rancher's boy from the back of the wagon.

"Get back or you'll end up like your friend."

"He's sick. You can't bring him into town. We'll all die!"

"We're taking him to Doc Wilson," Slocum said. His mind raced, trying to remember how many rounds he had fired. Four? He had only two shots left and faced a half dozen men. A quick look around convinced Slocum they would be in the middle of a crowd in seconds.

Josiah Jerrold understood the danger and whipped his team, getting the wagon rolling. Slocum trailed, swinging his six-gun around, hunting for the crowd's leader. The man still in the dust was as close as it came to someone leading them. The crowd was a giant headless monster writhing about and killing senselessly. There was no telling how many of them Slocum would have to kill before the rest even noticed. Fear drove them. Nothing but stark, gut-tearing fear.

He and Jerrold left the crowd behind and reached the doctor's office. The tent city had decreased in size. Slocum saw a newly built shed out back and realized that fewer men were in the makeshift ward. They had died.

Meghan came out, looking pale and drawn. Slocum doubted she had slept since he had been gone.

"You found him. Can he—?" Her bright eyes fixed on Josiah Jerrold, showing her hope and fear.

"You are as lovely as ever, my dear," Jerrold said reflex-ively.

"You don't have to sell her your devil's brew," Slocum said. "She wants it for her son."

"Frank's doing all right," Meghan said. She came to Slocum and looked up at him. She lowered her voice and said, "Thank you. The tonic is keeping him alive and so many others have died. More'n half who get it die, and the ones recovering aren't able to do much at all, being in such weakened conditions."

Slocum dismounted and went to the back of the wagon.

"Is there room inside for one more or should I put him in a tent?"

"The tent over there. Poor Mrs. Gossett died this morning. I . . . I tried to give her some of the tonic, but it was too late for her. If I'd shared sooner . . ."

"Don't," Slocum said sharply. "Frank is still alive. Now that Dr. Jerrold is here, others can get his potion. All of them, probably."

"Don't forget your role in obtaining the essential ingredients, son," Josiah Jerrold said. He helped as much as he could with the rancher's son, then stepped away and brushed his hands off on his coat. "I must get back to the formulation." He looked at Slocum, then at Meghan. "You, my dear, need to rest. All is well now that I have arrived."

"But Frank . . ." she started.

Dr. Wilson came from his office, looking even more exhausted than Meghan. His shirt hung open and a small leather bag dangled from around his neck. He saw Slocum's eyes fix on it.

"It can't hurt," Wilson said defensively. "Asafetida can't hurt."

Slocum scoffed. "Devil's dung."

"It's kept me from getting the diphtheria," Wilson said.

"That's because it smells so bad, nobody can get close enough to you to pass along the disease," Josiah Jerrold said, his nose crinkling up at the awful smell. "Come here and help me make more of my tonic." Wilson joined Jerrold, who stood on the back stage of his wagon and made shooing motions in Slocum and Meghan's direction. Then he pushed aside the curtain and disappeared to show Wilson how to concoct the medicine.

"I need to watch Frank."

Slocum followed her to the door of the office. Across the narrow room, half under the doctor's desk, lay Frank Mallory. When Slocum had left to find Jerrold, the boy had been perched on the brink of death. Color had now returned to his cheeks and he breathed evenly.

"His fever broke right after you rode out," Meghan said, tears in her eyes. "You saved him, John." She looked at him.

"Come on. You should get away from here. Frank's all right. Besides, there are two doctors to look after him now."

"I could use some rest," she said.

Slocum wrinkled his nose. "You can use a bath. You smell like a pigpen. Worse. You smell like Doc Wilson's asafetida."

"Not that!" Meghan said in mock horror. She laughed. Then she said, "I haven't felt like laughing in days. Thank you, John, thank you for everything."

Slocum stepped out into the tent city arrayed at the doctor's door. The patients in the tents ran the gamut from almost dead to barely ill. He wondered who the first would be to receive Jerrold's elixir. Keep the ones at the beginning stages from getting worse or try to pull back the worst from the brink of death? It was a moral decision he was glad he did not have to make.

He took Meghan by the arm and steered her away from the tents and past the shed where he knew the dead had been stacked like cordwood. The stench was getting so bad it might be best simply to set the shed on fire rather than wait for the undertaker to move the bodies out to the cemetery.

"I haven't been away since you left, John. I feel positively giddy at the fresh air."

Slocum felt the warmth of the sun on his face, and warmness elsewhere, too, being so close to Meghan. They were both filthy from their past few days' struggles, but he hardly noticed.

"There," he said, pointing. "The town bathhouse."

"You weren't joking about that, were you?" She looked at him, eyes bright. A smile curled the corners of her mouth.

"You're pretty, no matter what," he said, "but you're positively beautiful when you smile."

Before she could answer, he slid his arm around her waist and pulled her to him. They stared at each other for a moment. Slocum worried that she might resist, her husband being hardly in the ground a couple days, but she showed no hesitation. Meghan closed her eyes, tipped her head back, and he kissed her. For a moment the world stopped all around him. Their lips crushed and the kiss deepened.

When they broke off, Meghan leaned back, supported by Slocum's arm at the small of her back.

"I wondered if you'd be bold enough to kiss me again," she said.

"I'm bolder than that," Slocum said. Meghan stiffened, but he did not release her. She smiled almost shyly.

"Good," she said. "Let's go take that bath."

"I'll wash your back if you wash mine," Slocum said, feeling better than he had in weeks.

"Wash? Is that what you call it?"

Slocum slid his hands down to her buttocks and pulled her firmly into his body for another kiss. This seemed to last for an eternity, but when they broke off again, Slocum knew there was no turning back. She might be a widow and vulnerable, but it didn't matter. He knew what he wanted and from what he saw and tasted and felt, Meghan wanted the same thing.

They walked to the deserted bathhouse. While Meghan started a fire in the Franklin stove to one side of the small room, Slocum fetched water. He dumped the first few buckets into the high-backed galvanized tub, and by the time he returned with two more, Meghan had the fire going. Slocum put the water into a large pan on the top of the stove.

"No more, John," she said. "This will be enough to get us going."

He watched as she began unbuttoning her blouse. She knew how it excited him watching more and more of her snowy white flesh appear as the cloth pulled back. She tossed her blouse aside and stood naked to the waist. Stepping up, he took her breasts in his hands and squeezed just a little. Her blue eyes closed, and she moaned softly.

"I love the feel of your hands on me, John. I want to feel more. I want more!" As he fondled her, she reached down and gripped at his crotch. It was his turn to groan. She had found how hard he was, trapped behind the fly of his jeans.

He caught first one and then the other nipple between thumb and forefinger, twisting back and forth. The tiny pink nubs hardened as he toyed with them. He knew she had freed him from his gunbelt, because he stepped clear of it as he bent forward to suckle at one breast. He cupped the generous mound with his hand and applied his lips to the very tip.

The hardness between his lips began to throb with every frenzied beat of her heart. He sucked as much of the tit into his mouth as he could, then pushed it out slowly, using his tongue. When he had completed the unhurried, tantalizing oral trip on one breast, he repeated it on the other.

"I . . . I'm getting weak in the knees."

His arms went around her waist to support her. Then he stood and swung her around, her feet off the floor so he could bury his face in the deep valley between her breasts. She trembled with anticipation of his tongue and lips now. He blew gently on one nipple to cool it, then popped it back into his mouth.

"I'm burning up inside, John. I need you so!"

Slocum felt as if he might explode at any instant. He spun her around and put her on her feet next to the tub.

"Get naked," he ordered. "Entirely naked." He watched as she hastily obeyed, stepping away from her skirt to show herself entirely to him. "You're not beautiful, you're gorgeous. I've never seen a more gorgeous woman."

He skinned out of his shirt and kicked free of his boots as she turned and bent over slightly, presenting her firm rump to him when she took the pan of hot water from the stove. With a single quick toss, she added the boiling hot water to the tub. When it mixed with the cold water already there, the temperature would be about right.

"In," he said.

She widened her stance and ran her long fingers down to the thatch between her legs. "In," she said.

With a quick hop, she stepped into the tub and waited for him. Slocum hastily joined her. She pushed him down into the water so his back was propped against the tub, then straddled his waist and settled down. Slocum watched silently as she shimmied from side to side, her breasts jiggling. Her thighs spread and her knees disappeared under the warm water.

Then Slocum felt something more than warm all around him. Meghan closed her eyes and twisted slowly from side to side to get him settled deep within her.

"It's so big, John. So big. I'd forgotten what this is like."

He reached out and began playing with her breasts again. Meghan leaned forward to press herself harder into his hands. She continued tensing and relaxing all around his hidden manhood.

Slocum had wanted her. Now he had her and couldn't have been more aroused. His hands slid over her damp skin, stroking and arousing. He pressed here and there, then pinched and tweaked and gave Meghan as much enjoyment as he was receiving.

"I have to move more, faster, oh!"

She gasped as Slocum arched his back and drove himself a little farther into her heated center. He reached down underwater and stroked over her puckered pink nether lips as he continued moving. She crammed her hips down firmly to take even more of him into her depths as he stroked. Slocum reached around, grabbed a double handful of ass flesh and began guiding her in a faster, more insistent rhythm. He felt himself tensing, tightening, boiling inside.

"Yes, yes, yes," she sobbed out. He felt a ripple of desire pass through her body. Meghan tossed her head, long hair flying like a victory banner. Slocum gritted his teeth and kept moving. He felt the hot tide rising within, threatening to spill out. He was getting greedy and wanted more. He wanted as much of the willing, wanton woman as he could get.

Then there was no holding back. The feel of her sleek skin slipping wetly under his fingers, the way she surrounded him with a sheath of gripping, hot female flesh, the sloshing of warm water all around him—it all came together in a sudden rush. He pulled her forward and kissed her fervently as he spilled his seed. And then they melted into each other's arms, saying nothing and enjoying the warm afterglow.

He began running his hands up and down her back. When he found a bar of soap that had been left in the tub, he soaped her body and she let him explore her most intimate parts. Then she reciprocated. When they were both clean, they simply sat in the tub until the warm water turned tepid.

"We should get out," she said.

"We could heat more water. I might have missed a spot or two." Slocum tried to convince her by hunting for new sections of her thoroughly scrubbed body that he had missed.

"I'd like to, John, I would. But Frank . . ."

Slocum understood.

"Let me dry you off," he said.

"Only if I can dry you off, too," Meghan said. They climbed from the tub, found threadbare towels hanging from a hook near the stove, and took turns until both were dry. Slocum watched Meghan dress. She turned away shyly, as if there was something to hide after all they had just done. He didn't mind. The way she bent, her rump, nice and round and tight, was a sight not to be missed. And then it disappeared under the folds of her skirt.

Slocum strapped on his six-shooter and then spun, hand on the butt of his Colt when he heard gunfire out in the town.

"There are mobs prowling about everywhere," Meghan said. "They looted most of the stores. The only ones they didn't were watched over by their owners."

"How many got filled full of holes?"

"Not enough," Meghan said. Her hand covered her mouth as if she had said a bad word. "I didn't mean that. Not exactly. I don't want anyone killed."

Slocum couldn't agree. The looters all deserved to be strung up from the nearest sturdy oak tree limb. If there wasn't enough rope for them, he could find enough ammunition to do the job. Preying on the sick and dying was as low as a man could stoop.

Slocum took a quick look outside the bathhouse and them motioned for Meghan to follow. He walked quickly, every sense alert to trouble. The gunfire came from the far end of town, out near the bank or possibly the post office. Sentinel Butte would never be the same after the epidemic ran its course. With neighbor preying on neighbor, all trust would be gone.

That got him wondering about Meghan returning to her farm. What was there for a widow? She had to go back if her son lived, but what if Frank died? Slocum found himself thinking in ways that made him feel a bit guilty. It was one thing to look out for yourself and your interests, but it was something else wishing ill on others. Meghan might leave Sentinel Butte with him, but not as long as her son was alive. There was no life for a young boy drifting from town to town.

Slocum went into a crouch and brought up his six-shooter, aiming at barely seen movement along the roof of the bookstore next to the barbershop. When the man on the roof showed himself, Slocum fired.

"John, no!" cried Meghan.

"Wait here," he said, running to a water barrel, getting onto it, and then jumping to grab the edge of the roof. He pulled hard and skinned himself up and over the verge. He rolled onto the roof and got his footing. He kicked the man he had shot off onto the ground near Meghan, then picked up the torch the man had carried and dropped that into the rain barrel. It extinguished with a loud hiss and cloud of steam.

"He was going to set fire to the store," Slocum said.

"Oh, no," Meghan said in a small voice. "I didn't know. I thought you—" She closed her eyes, swallowed hard, then rushed to him and held him close when he dropped back to the street. "They're savages. He could have burned down the entire town!"

"That was probably what he wanted. Burn out the epidemic."

Together they returned to the doctor's office. Slocum looked around and went cold inside.

"Doc, Dr. Wilson!" he called.

The doctor poked his head out. "What's all the ruckus? I was trying to get some sleep."

"Where's Jerrold?"

"He left. He gave me all the leaves he'd collected and the recipe for boiling down the medicine. I'm dishing it out to the patients now." Wilson squinted and added, "Frank got some of the first batch, Miz Mallory. Seems fitting, the way Slocum here brought it all back with Dr. Jerrold and all."

Meghan hurried inside to see her son, leaving Slocum to stand out in the hot sun. He was sorry to see Josiah Jerrold leave, but he couldn't blame the snake oil peddler. Sentinel Butte was a dangerous place now.

As he started toward the main street to scout the progress made by the looters, Meghan ran back out.

"What's wrong?" he asked.

"It . . . it's making them worse, John. The medicine Jerrold brought back's making Frank and the others sicker. He's going into convulsions! He's going to die!"

11

"Now, you settle down, Miz Mallory. It's not that bad," Dr. Wilson said, coming from his office. He mopped his forehead with a dirty bandanna and looked around, as if hunting for men who might take a shot at him. Slocum knew there were some around town.

"But he's no better. He's shaking and crying out!"

"I gave him too much of the medicine," Wilson said, chewing on his lower lip. He looked hard at Slocum. "We've got to ration it since there's only so much that Josiah Jerrold brought, but it'll be enough."

"He's not better!"

Slocum went to the woman and took her aside. "Let the doctor work. He's been doing the best he can with the potion."

"He gave Frank some and it didn't do anything. It . . . it made him worse!"

"That's a far cry from it killing him. You made it sound like Frank was dying because of the medicine."

"He jerked all around. He wasn't doing that before. It's got to be the medicine. There's something wrong with it."

"Let me talk to the doctor," Slocum said, easing Meghan down into the shade where she could sit and fret. He motioned for Dr. Wilson to go inside. Wilson followed, sopping up sweat the whole way.

"I declare, if it gets any hotter, we'll all be dying of the heat and not diphtheria," he said once inside.

Slocum went to Frank Mallory's side. The boy looked paler than before. The color had drained from his cheeks and sweat beaded his forehead. Slocum put his hand there and felt the boy burning with fever. He looked up. Wilson shrugged.

"Don't know what happened. The boy was doing fine, then the fever came back. That happens. The course of a disease—any disease—is never in a straight line."

"Except when it's downhill and straight into a grave," Slocum said. He saw that two other patients in the room had died. "You give them Jerrold's elixir?"

"Some, not much. There wasn't much to go around considering how many patients I have. I wish he hadn't hightailed it like he did."

"Didn't he give you the formula?"

"Got it right here," Wilson said, rapping his knuckle on his desk. A slip of paper fluttered as he moved. "I don't have much of the leaves that seem to be a major ingredient."

"I can get more. I picked two bags' worth."

"Yeah, Jerrold told me. You were out on the Thompson ranch. Jerrold told me how old man Thompson tried to kill you and how you brought in Tom Junior."

"How's the boy doing?"

"Not so good. Might be he should have let you pick more of the plant."

"I'll get more, if you can use it to make more medicine."

"I'll run out of what I have by tomorrow. I cut back on how much I'm giving. Wish I knew the proper dosage. Will a little work or do I have to give each patient a gallon?"

"It didn't take much of the original batch," Slocum said, remembering how a couple teaspoons of the vile liquid had perked up Frank Mallory. "Why does it take more now?"

"Don't know that it does. It might be only a matter of how sick the patient is. I'm going to experiment some, giving a spoonful to those who are just coming down with the diphtheria and then the same to those who look like they're goners."

"Those two?"

Wilson shook his head when he saw Slocum had identified the two who had died. The doctor took a deep breath and said, "Will you help me move them to the shed? The undertaker's got more than his share of business to deal with, and he'd rather pretty up those with gunshots 'fore he buries them. Heaven alone knows there as many dying from lead poisoning as diphtheria."

Slocum heaved one man over his shoulder. The diphtheria had made the man waste away to little more than a bag of bones. Slocum swung the legs around and out the door. He heard rather than saw Meghan react. When she realized Slocum wasn't carrying her son, she settled back. He opened the shed door and almost gagged from the stench. Bottle flies buzzed around, and the corpses had become a free lunch for the maggots. It would be better to just set fire to the shed than wait for the undertaker to get around to dealing with the bodies.

Slocum added his burden to the pile and slammed the door.

He turned and ran into Meghan.

"The doctor told me he needs more of the plants. I want to help."

"Wilson needs all the help he can get here."

"It'll be for nothing if he doesn't have the leaves used to make the medicine. There's nothing else to do but make the afflicted comfortable until the die. I'd rather try to save them than make their final hours peaceful."

Slocum nodded. He understood. Sitting and watching the life drain was enough to drive anyone crazy. It would be worse for Meghan if her son slipped away. Doing something to help, even if she failed, was preferable.

"Get a horse saddled. Do you know anywhere we can find these?" Slocum poked around in a vest pocket and pulled out a lacy leaf he had tucked away during his first hunt.

"On my farm, no. But the hills above town might have some of it, up on Sentinel Butte. I don't know where, but this is something that'd grow in higher altitudes. It's adapted for cooler weather."

Slocum laughed. "You want to come along because it'll be cooler in the mountains and you want to get out of this heat?" Even breathing was like being underwater. He had been clean enough after their shared bath, but now his clothing again glued itself to his body because of sweat.

"I'll get one of the mules," she said.

"A horse. Find one. Steal it if you have to. We need to move faster than a mule can take us."

"All right. I'll ask Dr. Wilson."

"I'll find some more burlap bags for the leaves," Slocum said. He let her go rustle up a horse while he stepped out into the town's main street and looked around. The looters had turned the once-bustling street into a ghost town. He went directly to the general store. Stacked on the boardwalk out front were bags of potatoes. Slocum used his knife to slice open the top of the sacks so he could dump out the contents. The potatoes bounced and rolled all over, but he needed the bags, not the spuds. When he had six of the burlap bags, he figured that would be enough.

He had tucked them under his arm and started back for the doctor's office when he felt something. The hair on the back of his neck rose. His uncanny sense of danger had kept him alive during the war and it did so again. Slocum feinted right and dived left just as a shotgun barked. He felt one pellet scrape past his arm. He winced at the sudden pain and then hit the ground and rolled. He scrambled to get his six-shooter out. Flat on his back, he hunted for a target. Whoever had shot at him had done so from hiding.

Slocum listened hard and heard footsteps receding down an alley. He got to his feet and chased the bushwhacker down the narrow passage, and popped out behind the saloon in time to see a man trying to open a back door.

"Freeze," Slocum called, his pistol levelled.

"You—you're carryin' the plague. We gotta get rid of you and all the rest if we want to stay healthy." The man's pale face and the way his hands shook told Slocum it was too late. The disease had claimed another victim. This time it was affecting his brain.

"Drop the scattergun," Slocum said. "Drop it and let's go over to the doctor's office."

"You want to kill me. You're sick and you're gonna lock me up so I'll catch it and die!"

"No!" Slocum cried out as the man lifted the shotgun and pointed it in his direction. Slocum got off three shots before the man discharged his second barrel. All three hit the man in the chest, but none was fatal. The man dropped his shotgun and fell to his knees, clutching his chest. He looked up accusingly at Slocum.

"You done kilt me!"

"You're not dead yet," Slocum said. He approached warily, then holstered his six-gun and grabbed the man before he toppled onto his face. Pulling him to his feet, Slocum shifted the man's weight around, slung him over his shoulder, and headed for the doctor's office. It would be nip and tuck whether the bullets or the diphtheria claimed the man's life, but Slocum had done all he could.

"John, I heard shots." Meghan stepped back as he swung the wounded man around and dropped him onto a pallet in the closest tent. "Your shirt. Is . . . is that your blood?"

Slocum looked and saw that his shirt had been soaked with blood.

"Not mine," he said laconically. He pointed to the fallen man when Dr. Wilson came out. The doctor heaved a deep sigh and set to work. Slocum backed off and turned to face Meghan.

"You still want to ride with me?"

"Yes!" She gripped him fiercely, pressing her cheek against his shirt. He pushed her back.

"You'll get blood on you," he said. "I'll put on my other shirt."

He handed her the burlap bags and worked through his saddlebags until he found the faded red-and-black checked flannel shirt that served as his winter clothing. Wearing flannel in this weather would force him to drink even more water to keep from passing out. So be it. What Meghan had said about the plant growing in cooler altitudes was right, but it wasn't going to be that much cooler.

He stuffed his bloody shirt back into the saddlebags and mounted. Meghan waited for him, her face grim. Tears again stained her cheeks, but she didn't complain.

"I asked around. There might be a patch of those plants up there." She pointed up into the hills above the town of Sentinel Butte.

Slocum rode off at a brisk gait. Meghan trailed and finally got her horse to match his.

"How much do we need to harvest?" she asked.

"I got two bags before. Doc Wilson said he was running out fast, so let's get three times as much. Each of us can get three bags."

"I'm sorry, John."

He looked at her. Tears ran unashamedly down her cheeks.

"What are you apologizing for?"

"Being so weak. Being so concerned about my son. Knowing you're our only salvation and—"

"Frank is all you should worry about, and the leaves will boil down and give him all the medicine he needs."

She nodded, but the tears kept running down her cheeks. They rode in silence for several miles, until Meghan pointed to a trail meandering up into the hills.

"Up there's likely to be our best chance."

Slocum studied the steep trail. He didn't see any of the special plant growing along it, but that meant nothing. All he had found before had been in broad, grassy meadows where the plants could get plenty of sunlight and rain. This steep a trail would cause the water to run off during any rainstorm.

Slocum started up the trail, letting Meghan trot along behind. He listened hard for any hint that they might not be alone. Too many times the looters and those driven crazy by diphtheria had tried to waylay him. He looked over his shoulder. Meghan steadfastly rode, determined now not to be any burden to him. She was about the only one Slocum wanted to waylay him, but that would have to be later.

Until then he could remember the time they'd shared and consider what the future might hold for them. For Slocum this was new territory to explore. Planning with him didn't usually go past deciding what to bag and cook for dinner. If he wanted to plan a long way in the future, he'd choose some distant destination and ride there. Beyond this, he was hardly more than a leaf caught in a wayward wind.

Since meeting Meghan, he'd felt as if he was caught up in a tornado spinning him all around.

"There, John. Is that a patch?"

"Yup." He dismounted and opened a bag. He stuffed the leaves in willy-nilly.

"You don't know the first thing about harvesting herbs, do you?" She dismounted and joined him. She drew a short-bladed kitchen knife. "Watch." She began cutting the leaves with deft strokes of the small blade. Slocum watched as she collected twice as many leaves as he had, in a fraction of the time.

"You don't get the sap on your hands, either," he said. He drew his heavier knife and went to work, hacking as if he used a scythe. This brought a chuckle from Meghan. He was happy to see her mood lightening. And he was equally happy to see that her method worked well. He had a half bag collected by the time the patch was completely denuded.

"The plants would grow uphill and that way," Meghan said, studying the terrain. "Rain, light—those are what this plant needs most to prosper. Some of the forest plants don't hardly need sunlight. These, though, these need a lot of sun."

Slocum let her ramble on with her lecture about the plants because it kept her mind occupied with thoughts other than her son dying.

"What are you going to do? After the epidemic's over?"

He had been listening with only half an ear as they continued to collect the plants, and it took him a few seconds to realize she had moved on from trivial talk to something that affected him. Both of them.

"I'll decide when I get there," he said.

"You're not much for worrying over the future, are you?"

"The here and now fills up my time," he said. Slocum wondered why he felt so uncomfortable telling her what he had really been thinking. Meghan obviously had the same things on her mind as he did. What would *they* do when the diphtheria faded into memory?

"Yes, I suppose it does. Do we have enough?"

"The patch isn't that far from town. We can come back if this isn't enough," he said.

"We've collected four sacks for the doctor. That's twice what Dr. Jerrold brought back."

Slocum and Meghan rode back to town, an uneasy silence between them.

12

"He's not getting better," Meghan said. "Why isn't he?"

"These things take time," Dr. Wilson said, looking worried. "He is making progress, yes, definitely that. At least, he's no worse than he was yesterday."

"But you've given him the medicine. You made it up according to Dr. Jerrold's formula. I saw you. I read it aloud for you while you worked. What's wrong? Frank isn't getting better."

"You're distraught. I'd give you some laudanum to quiet your frazzled nerves, but I've run out. Some of the patients needed it to ease their way into a better place." Wilson looked anxiously at Slocum for help with the woman.

Slocum considered letting the doctor flounder about, then went to Meghan and said quietly, "You're not going to do your boy any good if you wear yourself out."

"Why haven't I gotten diphtheria? Why haven't either of you?" Her nose wrinkled at the smell of Wilson's asafetida bag. No one, least of all the doctor, really thought that prevented him from catching the disease. Still, he wore it like some badge of his profession.

"I've seen army companies where everyone but a single soldier got dysentery, most of them dying. Why didn't the one soldier? There's no way to know," Slocum said. "You've got to rest so you can nurse your son back to health."

He led her away. Meghan was too distraught, approaching exhaustion, to fight him any more. Slocum got her outside and steered her toward a tent where a half dozen pallets stretched abandoned and empty. He had personally washed the blankets after the patients who had lain on them died. All six of them had been given the new batch of Jerrold's elixir, and it hadn't done squat for any of them.

"Lie down and rest. I'll be back in a few minutes. Rest," Slocum said sternly. Meghan was too tired to protest. She lay back on the blankets and in seconds was asleep. Slocum watched. She might not be asleep as much as simply passed out from fatigue.

He went back into the doctor's office and confronted the man.

"Why isn't it working?" he demanded. "The potion hasn't helped a single one of the people you gave it to. The earlier bottles worked, and these don't."

"I can't say what's wrong. I followed Jerrold's instructions to the letter. More than once, actually." Wilson closed his eyes and rubbed them with both fists. He was as close to collapse as Meghan, but Slocum wasn't letting him rest until he got answers.

"Was it the wrong plant?"

"It was the same. Not only did you have the one leaf in your pocket, Jerrold furnished a dried one to use as an example so there wouldn't be any mistake." The doctor yawned widely. "I did everything right. It just didn't work this time."

"Something was different. If all the ingredients were the same, maybe the method Jerrold used to brew it up was different."

"I don't know, Slocum. It might be he used different equipment or brewed for a different time or temperature or who the hell knows? He made a medicine that worked. I didn't." Wilson collapsed into the chair behind his desk. He wobbled a little, then put his head on his crossed arms. He was asleep as quickly as Meghan.

Slocum stared at the snoring physician and then turned away. He knew what had to be done. Josiah Jerrold had left to keep from catching diphtheria. Slocum had to track him down again and find out if the patent medicine peddler had done anything to whip up his first batch that he hadn't mentioned in his instructions. There didn't seem to be any hope for those with the disease if some small step, some tiny difference in preparation, wasn't discovered.

It took him the better part of an hour to get supplies for the trail. He made certain he had plenty of ammo, not only for hunting but for keeping the looters and roving bands of thieves at bay. Jerrold would have driven due west again, this time probably not deviating from the road but pressing on, maybe to the town along the southwestern fork or maybe just going directly across the prairie stretching along the base of the mountains. Wherever he went, Slocum intended to track him down and find the real secret to the potion.

Even if Josiah Jerrold didn't realize there *was* a real secret, Slocum would find what it was.

Slocum approached the three wagons slowly, making sure he didn't look too threatening. For two days he hadn't seen any other riders, but there was no telling what these settlers might have encountered. Three men stood with rifles in hand, watching him suspiciously. He remembered the other wagon train he had come across and how those folks had been rightfully uneasy around strangers.

"Hello!" Slocum took off his hat and wiped his face, giving them time to see who he was. The three men huddled, discussed the matter, then split apart so they could get him in a cross fire if it came to shooting. Slocum hoped it wouldn't. He was tired from so much riding and wanted only to find Josiah Jerrold and his medicine wagon.

"What kin we do fer ya?"

"I'm looking for a friend. Drives a wagon all painted up with signs. Dr. Josiah Jerrold, he calls himself."

"What do you want with him?"

"He's a friend, and I got some powerful important news to tell him. He's needed back in Sentinel Butte."

"There's sickness in that town," muttered the man on the far right. "You say this gent you're lookin' fer's a doctor?"

"That he is. He drives a medicine wagon. Says so on the side."

"You don't mean him harm?"

"It's important that he get back to Sentinel Butte," Slocum said. "Reckon I'd give my life so he could. Have you seen him?"

"Only this morning. He took a cutoff not five miles back along this road, angling up into the hill country."

Slocum wiped more sweat from his face, then took a long drink from his canteen. When he was done, he asked, "Anything I can do for you folks? If not, much obliged for the information. It might save some lives."

Slocum waited a few seconds. If they had lied to him, this was their opportunity to change their minds and give him the truth. From what he could tell of the three men, they had been truthful. None of them had so much as batted an eye when their leader told Slocum how Josiah Jerrold had gone into the hills. He touched the brim of his hat, wheeled his horse around, and cut across country. If Jerrold followed the road, Slocum could cut off a couple hours of tracking. The wagon would never make it off the trail he had seen, which would keep the patent medicine peddler moving along real slow.

Slocum hadn't ridden a mile when he got the uneasy feeling of being spied on. He drew rein and looked around.

The open countryside didn't afford much in the way of
hiding places for a would-be spy. There were deep ravines
that carried spring runoff from the mountains, but not much
else. A mile or two ahead the gentle slope leading into hill-
ier country was spotted with scrubby trees. No place for
anyone to hide.

Slocum reached into his saddlebags and pulled out his
field glasses. A slow survey of the country ahead of him
made him smile. He'd been being too edgy. He spotted
Jerrold's wagon pulled off the road, probably near a stream
to water his team.

As he lowered the glasses, though, he got another cold
chill that ran up and down his spine. Something was wrong,
very wrong. Using the binoculars again, he tried to find
Jerrold anywhere around the wagon. That he didn't wasn't
too unusual. Jerrold might be inside brewing up more of his
potions to sell at his next stop, or he could be out scouring
the countryside for more herbs. The old man might even be
asleep in the wagon.

But Slocum knew Jerrold wasn't the problem. He continued slowly scanning the country. A tiny reflection of sunlight
off metal stopped him. He sat astride his increasingly nervous mare and tried to make out who was trying to hide.

The glint of sunlight came more clearly. Slocum tucked
away his field glasses and turned his horse away from
where Jerrold had camped. He needed to fetch the patent
medicine peddler back to Sentinel Butte, but riding directly
to him wasn't possible.

The reflection Slocum had seen had been the sun shin-
ing off a marshal's badge.

He snapped the reins and got his mare trotting along, retracing his path. He wasn't sure the marshal had spotted
him, but he couldn't take any chances. The fate of an entire
town depended on him reaching Josiah Jerrold and finding
what the man had done to the earlier batch of medicine that

he hadn't done to the one he'd left for Dr. Wilson to administer.

Finding a deep ravine, Slocum urged his horse down the crumbling embankment to the sandy bottom. Although the sandy bottom, strewn with rocks, some the size of his fist, slowed him, he had no choice but to follow the deep gully. Staying out of sight was the only way he was going to carry his message to Jerrold.

Slocum drew rein when he saw two riders in the gully ahead. A quick tug on the reins reversed direction. He started back the way he had come. The going was easier since the downslope didn't tax his mare's strength. He still worried about how effective Jerrold's liniment had been at healing the horse's leg. There hadn't been any trouble since he had removed the liniment-soaked bandage, but Slocum knew the injury could recur at any instant. If it did, he would be stranded and unable to escape.

"Damn," he muttered. He began to worry about escaping at all now that he was in the bottom of the streambed. Two riders blocked his way up into the hills, and now he saw three more appear on the left edge of the ravine. Hiding was out of the question.

Slocum kept riding, trying to ignore them. He might be able to bluff his way to freedom.

All chance of that disappeared when he rounded a bend and saw three men waiting in the ravine bottom. Their six-shooters were drawn and aimed in his direction. The range was so great that hitting him would be a matter of luck and not skill.

But he had nowhere to run.

Seeing an eroded section in the side of the deep ravine sent a thrill of hope through him. He urged his horse into the narrow channel and upward, getting out of the streambed. He had half the posse behind him, but if he reached a forested area, he knew he could lose them. Their tracker would have to be an Apache to follow his spoor if Slocum set his mind to it.

He never got the chance to reach the woods.

"Hold up there," called the federal marshal. "We got you dead to rights." He lifted the rifle to his shoulder and sighted at Slocum. Even at this range, the bore looked like it was big enough to crawl into.

"I got to see the medicine man up on the hillside," Slocum called. "It's a matter of life and death."

"The only death'll be yours, you no-account road agent!" Slocum saw no way to run and no need to make his dying easy for the federal marshal. He raised his hands slowly, knowing that more than Frank Mallory would die if he didn't get word to Jerrold to return to Sentinel Butte.

Slocum just hoped the marshal didn't have an itchy trigger finger.

"I surrender!" he called.

"That's a damn shame," the lawman said. "I had my heart set on plugging you. But the day's young. I might still get the chance."

The posse rode up behind Slocum and from the left. With armed men on three sides, he had no chance at all to run—and live.

13

"Talk to him. Give him my message. You've got to get Jerrold to return to Sentinel Butte!"

"This is some kinda trick, ain't it?" The federal marshal scowled at Slocum. "I seen it all, so you're not gettin' any of my posse to stick their feet into a bear trap."

"Yeah," piped up a young man, probably not out of his teens, but feeling full of piss and vinegar because he wore a deputy's badge on his chest, "we seen it all. You figger he'd be sendin' us into an ambush?"

"Might be," allowed the marshal.

"Should we go arrest that son of a bitch, too? Me and a couple of the boys kin circle him and get the drop on him 'fore he knows what's going on."

"No need. We know this was the only one who tried to hold up the stage," the marshal said. "He's the one what sprung my trap, and he's the one that will go to jail for it. I figger you good for ten years once the jury hears all the evidence and the judge understands what a menace to civilized man you are. If I kin find any more broken laws to pin on you—say, a wanted poster or two—why, you might be in prison longer than that."

"There's an epidemic raging," Slocum said. "Dr. Jerrold can slow it down."

"I know all about this here epidemic. Ain't the plague, like some of the folks I talked to are sayin'," the marshal said. "I seen plenty of that when I was in New Orleans right after the war. Dangedest thing I ever did see. Rats dancin' along the wharf. Dancin' with the black plague. Drives 'em crazy, I reckon."

"This is diphtheria. The doctor in Sentinel Butte said so."

"Never been through a plague of that," the deputy said, riding a little farther from Slocum. "You been exposed?"

"Yes," Slocum said, noting that the rest of the posse drifted away, too, all except the marshal. He had his prisoner, and even fear of diphtheria wouldn't force him to give up this close to victory.

The movement wasn't enough for Slocum to make a break. The marshal had taken his six-shooter and rifle and was cagey enough not to risk having his prisoner escape.

"You been out hunting me for long?" Slocum finally asked.

"Enough to make me real anxious about gettin' back to where I kin get a decent meal and a warm bed." The marshal smirked. "Got me a woman, too, wantin' to warm more'n her side of the bed."

"You're looking a mite peaked, Marshal," Slocum said, studying the man intently.

"Don't go playin' mind games with me. I'm tired from bein' on the trail after you, that's all."

Slocum wasn't so sure. He had seen enough patients, both in Sentinel Butte and out on the prairie, to recognize the symptoms. The marshal hardly noticed, but he wobbled as he rode and his leathery skin was paler than usual, if Slocum was any judge. A man riding under the harsh Dakota sun wouldn't be tending toward the paleface.

"Just saying," Slocum said. "Where you taking me?"

"There's a nothing of a town a mile or two ahead, but

it's got a jail," the marshal said. "Don't even remember the name. You remember, Leroy?"

The young deputy screwed up his face as he concentrated, then shook his head.

"Don't matter. We'll just have you there overnight while we take a break 'fore headin' back to Fargo. If I find a telegraph along the way—they got one in this town, Leroy?"

"Don't recall seein' poles or wires, much less a wire road," Leroy said.

"When I reach somewhere that'll let me send a telegram, I'll let 'em know back in Fargo to start celebratin'."

"Bet there ain't been no more robberies since we caught him," Leroy said.

The marshal ignored his wet-behind-the-ears deputy and said, "There'll be a goodly reward on your head. I kin feel it."

"What else can you feel, Marshal? A cold sweat?"

The lawman flared. "You shut yer mouth or I'll gag you."

Slocum saw the way the marshal had to fight to keep in the saddle. It was more than trail dust and bad cooking that had gotten to him. Slocum knew better than to harp on the subject of the epidemic. If the marshal had caught diphtheria, getting away would be easier along the trail. The marshal might even send his whole posse back so he and his deputy could bring in their notorious prisoner and claim all the glory. If that happened, Slocum knew he could get away. The marshal ill, the deputy stupid, escape was possible.

"There's the town. Hardly enough buildings, but they got a saloon," the deputy said.

"You don't go gettin' knee-walkin' drunk like you done back in Bismarck, now, Leroy."

"Aw, Marshal, it weren't that bad."

"It was," the marshal said firmly. "But you and the rest of the boys go wet your whistles. I'll be along as soon as I check our guest into the gray bar hotel." That provoked a loud cheer for the marshal. The posse galloped off and hit the ground running in their attempt to see who would be the first into the saloon.

Slocum was more interested in who the last one out would be and that man's condition then.

"He's a damn fine tracker. Ain't got a lick of sense, but Leroy's got a nose like a bloodhound. That's why I keep him around."

"What's he to you? Cousin?"

"Brother-in-law," the marshal said. He stiffened when he realized he had answered. He mopped at his forehead and looked a shade paler. The disease was beginning to eat away at him, and he was only beginning to notice.

"You can save yourself some trouble and let me go, Marshal."

"I kin save the territory some money and string you up here and now," the marshal snapped. "Git down."

Slocum stepped down and swung the reins around a hitching post.

"You going to take care of my horse?"

"I . . . I'll put her in the livery and give 'er some grain," the marshal said. He braced himself on the railing, then motioned for Slocum to precede him into the jail.

The town marshal looked up, eyes wide when he saw he had visitors.

"Sully, you old son of a bitch. What you bringin' me?"

The marshal shoved Slocum forward. "A road agent who thought he could outrun me and the boys. A whole posse was needed to track this one down. He's slipperier than a rainbow trout in a mountain stream."

"I'll keep him on ice for you," the town marshal said. "How long?"

"Daybreak tomorrow, I intend to ride out. Might send the rest of the boys on home since it's been a week or so since they were . . ." The marshal frowned. He had lost his train of thought.

Slocum hoped the town marshal wouldn't comment on it. The sicker the marshal got, the more likely he was to let his prisoner escape.

"Make yerse'f at home," the town marshal said. "How 'bout you and me gettin' a drink, Sully?"

"Need food more. That restaurant still open at the far end of town?"

"The one with the cute li'l waitress? You bet. I think she's got her cap set for me, but she's playin' coy."

"Coy," Sully said. He swiped at more sweat on his forehead and shivered a little. "I need food bad. Can't remember when I ate last."

"You ought to teach that no-account brother-in-law of yours to cook somethin' more'n a mess of beans."

The cell door clanged shut behind Slocum, and the two lawmen left him alone. Slocum sat for a few minutes, studying how the cell was put together. He waited a respectable length of time to be sure the lawmen didn't return to check on him. Once they'd ordered and gotten their food, they'd be less likely to take the time to look in.

When he was sure they were eating at the diner—and his belly rumbled at the thought of them wolfing down food—he went to the cell door and laid his hands against it, as if pressing with his palms might spring the lock.

The door was stronger than that. Slocum doubted a horse could pull the door off, but he didn't stop at only examining the lock or hinges. He sidled along the thick steel bars until he came to the wall where bolts had been driven into a wood frame to hold the cell together. Time and high humidity had rotted the wood. Slocum began digging at the bottom bolt, until he had a small pile of wood splinters on the floor. He checked again to be sure he wasn't likely to be interrupted, then dropped to the floor, braced his back against the cot, and used both feet to shove hard.

He grunted with exertion. The wood tore away a bit. He doubled his efforts. More wood. He felt the bars beginning to yield. With a convulsive shove that drained him of energy, he forced the bottom bolts on the bars free of the rotted wood. He got his breath, pushed some more and made an opening of a few inches between iron bar and frame. Worming his shoulders past was all it took. He lost skin as he finally got free of the cell, but he didn't care. He was on the right side of the bars now.

Slocum fetched his Colt Navy and knife and settled them at his waist and in the top of his right boot. A quick look outside showed the town coming alive—or as much as the tiny farming town ever could. Raucous music slipped out the saloon's front door and men inside sang along. Other than this, nothing stirred.

He slipped free, saw that his horse was gone, and panicked for a moment. Then he thought. Marshal Sully struck him as an honest man. He'd said he would see to Slocum's horse. Finding the livery stables wasn't difficult, and Slocum grinned. The lawman had kept his word. The mare had been curried and fed, and she stood patiently.

It was the work of minutes to saddle and ride from town. Slocum had to wait for thick clouds to clear enough for him to get a decent view of the stars and his bearings. Josiah Jerrold was somewhere north of here, and it was past time that Slocum herded the peddler back to Sentinel Butte.

Slocum wished he hadn't tried to convince the marshal to give Jerrold the message about returning to the center of the epidemic. This route might be the first direction the marshal looked. Slocum wasn't sure he believed Sully when he said his brother-in-law was that good a tracker, but balancing the need for speed with caution occupied Slocum's attention for more than a mile.

The decision came quickly. He didn't want to believe it, but he had to consider that the marshal was right about his deputy's abilities. Rather than make a beeline back north, Slocum cut west, found a sluggishly running stream, and followed it for a mile. When he exited the water, he hacked off some sage and tied a rock to it along with his rope.

Dragging it behind to hide his tracks wasn't that good a ploy. A decent tracker would notice the drag marks and the occasional hoofprint, but it was something Slocum could do easily. If the deputy was as good as Sully claimed, Slocum would lead them off a cliff. He found a rockier patch of ground and kept riding straight, being sure the drag marks and bits of sage torn free from the bush were obvious. If it didn't rain and the wind didn't blow too hard, the posse was likely to keep going in a straight line, thinking Slocum had done the same.

He turned right and headed directly north again, then angled back, following a ravine. The sandy bottom made walking difficult, but the shifting sand didn't hold a hoofprint well. Another sluggishly flowing stream, bigger than before, led Slocum due north, in the direction he wanted.

By sunrise, he was tired, but he knew he had done the best he could to hide his trail. If the marshal hadn't figured out his prisoner had flown the coop, he would soon. Slocum tried to guess what Sully would do. He still had his posse. Mention of Sentinel Butte hadn't been too smart, but Slocum had been desperate and had momentarily hoped the marshal would bend and go see what was happening there. The town was likely where the posse would head. All he could hope for was their fear of disease being stronger than their need to set a trap for him.

Slocum wasn't so sure about the marshal. He had the look of a man too sick to ride. That might make finding Jerrold easier, without the tenacious marshal after him, but sending Jerrold to Sentinel Butte would require caution. Slocum didn't dare ride in with him, or the posse might nab him again.

He'd cross that stream when he came to it.

Dizzy himself from exhaustion and not getting any food more than a bit of moldy jerky he gnawed while in the saddle, Slocum rode hard until he found the area where he had been captured. A quick survey of the terrain and he focused in on where he had seen Jerrold's gaudily painted wagon parked beside a stream. When he found the spot, he dropped down and studied the tracks.

"What are you doing, you crazy galoot?" The tracks went due north into the mountains—and Indian country.

14

"Dammit, Jerrold, don't you ever look around to see what's going on?" Slocum walked his horse as he followed the tracks left by the medicine wagon. He knew he had the right trail because alongside the twin ruts through the increasingly mountainous terrain someone had neatly clipped plants. Some had been pulled up by their roots, while others had been surgically pared, leaves from stems. Only Josiah Jerrold would collect plant specimens like this.

Slocum cursed some more under his breath when he found a turkey feather. He picked it up and examined it in the late afternoon sunlight. He saw where it had been notched for insertion into a headband. The Indian scout trailing Jerrold for more than two miles had lost it. The scene was as clear to Slocum as if he'd watched it with his own eyes. Jerrold had clanked and rattled along in his wagon, and the brave had been less than a hundred yards back at times. For whatever reason, the brave had ducked and caught the feather on a low-hanging tree limb off to one side of the road. The feather had come loose, and the Indian, intent on watching Jerrold's progress, had not noticed.

Slocum angrily threw the feather away. Any brave sporting one feather might wear others, showing his fighting prowess. One feather for each enemy killed in battle. Would a brave gain another feather for taking Jerrold's scalp?

The notion made Slocum smile grimly. There was hardly enough hair on the top of the peddler's head to make it worthwhile. More likely, the brave would count coup and then kill Jerrold. There wasn't much in the wagon the Sioux would want to steal, but there might be some food and other items they could barter. The blankets would be the first to go, and Jerrold's team. Otherwise, Slocum expected to see the abandoned wagon with every turn he took in the steep mountain road.

He kept walking, every step heavy, as if his feet had been dipped in lead. Finding Jerrold was imperative if Dr. Wilson wanted more of the potion that worked to hold back the ravages of the disease, but finding the man alive seemed less and less likely.

"Damn," Slocum said. He dropped to his knees and brushed away dirt to show where a second brave had joined the first. Jerrold might have held off one warrior, but two was out of the question. The Sioux were simply too fierce for that.

The narrow road plastered to the side of the hill would have made turning the wagon impossible, save for occasional broadening in the road. Where it led was a mystery, since Slocum had never heard of a town in this direction, but then he hadn't known about the small town where Marshal Sully had tried to lock him up. The way the settlers spread across the western Dakotas might be impossible to keep up with even living here. For a drifter like Slocum, who passed through only every few years, the rise of the towns was like a minor miracle.

He studied the road a bit more and decided this had been a mining road some time back. The silver mines had played out, and the road had fallen into disuse. Jerrold hadn't headed for a town. So why the hell was he going this way at all? Slocum couldn't answer that. Jerrold didn't strike him as the kind of man who got lost easily. He had a nose for selling his patent medicines, and the only place to do that was in a town bustling with citizens who didn't know they were sick until offered a bottle of elixir. Going to a working mine might serve the same purpose, but even Jerrold must have noticed the condition of the road.

Nobody had driven along this road in months. There weren't even signs of horseback riders—except the Sioux braves.

Slocum mounted and urged his mare to greater speed. Jerrold might hold off two braves, but he couldn't do that for long. If Slocum attacked from the rear, he stood a small chance of saving Jerrold. Catching the Indians in a cross fire wouldn't be anything they'd anticipated.

The slope evened out, and Slocum found himself riding into a mountain meadow. He almost cried out when he saw Jerrold's wagon making its way directly across the grassy terrain. He clamped his mouth tightly shut when he saw the two braves appear from a shallow ravine and gallop directly toward Jerrold.

Slocum could not hope to reach the man in time, and the distance was far too great for a shot, even if he had the old sniper rifle he used during the war. His Winchester carbine had too short a barrel for such an accurate shot from this distance.

Slocum watched the braves separate and approach the wagon from opposite sides. One Sioux disappeared, but Slocum still had a good view of the one on the right side of Jerrold's wagon.

The wagon stopped and the brave trotted over bold as brass. Slocum frowned. He wondered what had happened. The Indian made no move to draw either knife or pistol. Slocum waited for the report from the other brave's rifle. He waited—and it never came.

As he watched, the first brave motioned ahead and the wagon began rolling. For a brief moment Slocum saw both

Sioux warriors, one on either side of the wagon, and then they and Jerrold vanished down a gradual slope toward a river running the length of the meadow.

Slocum rubbed his lips with his sleeve as he considered what to do. The Indians hadn't killed Josiah Jerrold outright. That meant they had plans for him. How long he would last as their prisoner was another matter. Whatever he did, Slocum knew it had to be done fast.

How he would rescue Jerrold and get him away from the Sioux was a poser, but he hoped the doctor could ride bareback. There was no way in hell they could ever drive his medicine wagon out of the Sioux camp.

Slocum mounted and entered the meadow, wary of lookouts. His nose wrinkled when he caught the scent of cooking meat. As he rode, he turned slowly, focusing in on the delicious odor. His belly rumbled and his mouth began watering. Before he had reached the spot where Jerrold and the braves had disappeared, he saw thin wisps of smoke spiraling into the evening sky. Finding the Sioux camp was the easy part.

How could he ever hope to free Jerrold?

The wagon's tracks were plain in the soft earth, and Slocum followed them until he saw where they vanished into the woods on the far side of the meadow. He veered away and slipped into the forest. He tethered his horse, fixed the location in his mind the best he could, then advanced clutching his rifle. Moving like a shadow, he approached the Sioux camp—and was almost caught by the sentry posted in a tree above him.

A bit of bark fell on Slocum, warning him. He feinted left and spun right, forcing the falling Indian to miss his intended target. The brave landed on his feet in a crouch, but he had to balance with one hand against the ground. This prevented him from stabbing upward with the knife held in his other hand.

Slocum swung his rifle butt and caught the man on the

chin, snapping his head back. The Sioux fell heavily, thrashing about and trying to call out. Slocum wrested the knife from the brave's grip and used it with a single quick slash that sent blood spewing.

Panting harshly, Slocum rocked back, then threw down the bloodied knife. He wiped the spatter off his flannel shirt the best he could and picked up his rifle to continue the fight, if necessary. As fierce as the struggle had been, it had also been quick and relatively silent. No one in the Sioux camp had heard and grown suspicious.

Slocum dragged the dead brave away, found a shallow ravine, and rolled him into it. A rotting log and some leaves hid the body from all but the most intense search. Only then did Slocum return to spy on the camp. He had been fast, but how long did it take a Sioux to slit the throat of a captive? Jerrold might be dead and his body cooling in the still night.

Working closer to the camp, Slocum counted eight cooking fires. He had found a large Sioux encampment, maybe twenty or more braves and their squaws. The Indians must have felt secure to camp here, because if whatever mines nearby had closed, the white man had no reason to wander through this country now. The Sioux had regained control of their own land, at least until more settlers came and pushed them deeper into the mountains.

Slocum caught his breath when he saw the medicine wagon parked away from the camp. In the deepening shadows, he couldn't tell if Jerrold was there, but he saw no movement. Skirting the camp, making a wide circle around the joking, laughing Sioux warriors, Slocum dropped to his belly and inched forward toward the wagon. The team was still hitched. Slocum counted that as a good sign. While they weren't simply going to drive out of camp, this meant the Indians hadn't stolen the horses outright after killing Jerrold.

The patent medicine peddler might still be alive.

Senses straining for the slightest hint of trouble ahead, Slocum made his way to a point directly behind the wagon. He had started to push aside the curtain and look inside when voices behind him warned of danger. He dived under the wagon, rolled onto his back, and aimed his rifle toward the rear, where moccasins appeared. Two braves. They stood yammering in Sioux, arguing if Slocum caught the tone right, and one shoved the other. Their voices grew louder. Slocum held his breath. If others came, they were sure to spot him under the wagon.

Worse, the horses were growing restive from the argument raging at the rear. Slocum was just about ready to take matters into his own hands and see if he couldn't kill both braves before anyone else in the camp noticed, when the voices died down. The two men came closer, and whatever they had argued about was put aside. He watched as they disappeared into the darkness. He heaved a sigh of relief and scooted back to the rear of the wagon.

As he pushed aside the curtain with the barrel of his rifle, he knew what he would see.

He heaved another sigh of relief. The whole time he had hidden under the wagon, he hadn't heard so much as a creak or squeak above his head. That meant Jerrold was either dead or somewhere else. The small rolling laboratory was empty. The dark within might have confounded him, but he made sure. Empty.

He looked around, wondering where the Sioux would keep a prisoner like Jerrold. Another fighter would be tortured, but Josiah Jerrold was anything but that. Dropping to hands and knees, Slocum studied the ground until he found Jerrold's boot prints going off into the dark. Two Indians accompanied the doctor, whether as guards or something more, Slocum could not tell.

He hurried away from the camp, doing his best to follow the tracks. Just as he was certain he had lost the trail, he heard a low chanting ahead and smelled a pungent aroma that made his nose wrinkle. He threw caution to the winds and almost burst into the small clearing. In the center sat a medicine man in full regalia, tossing pinches of herbs into a fire. Behind him stood Josiah Jerrold with open jars of those herbs.

As the medicine man chanted, Jerrold handed different chemicals to him.

Slocum stepped away into deeper shadow, but the movement drew Jerrold's attention. His eyes widened and he started to speak. He clamped his mouth shut and continued to give the medicine man new herbs to toss into the fire. Some flared, others produced blue and green flames. All the while, the medicine man sat stolidly, eyes closed, face raised to the sky, and tossed into the fire whatever Jerrold handed him.

Jerrold bent low and spoke for several minutes, then placed the jars to the medicine man's right side where he could reach them easily. He stepped back, skirted the fire, and left the circle of light near where Slocum hid.

"What the bloody hell are you doin' here, son? You'll get yourself killed!"

"I came for you."

"That's about the dumbest thing I ever did hear."

"You're not their prisoner?"

"Of course not. That's Big Elk, the best of the Sioux medicine shaman. There's nothing he don't know about plants, minerals, or medicines. I come by here every year or so to swap recipes with him."

"You're one of the tribe?"

"Reckon you might say that. Big Elk's a powerful force in the tribe. All the war chiefs listen to him because he claims he can read the future."

"Using your potions?"

"Something like that," Jerrold said, chuckling. "It was from him I got the formula for the medicine I left in Sentinel Butte to help fight the diphtheria."

Slocum quickly explained how that formula hadn't worked.

"Do tell?" Jerrold pursed his lips, then shook his head. "Must be something I put in the first batch that I didn't remember. That's a shame."

"Why can't you just try a little bit of everything? There're men and women dying back there."

"And a boy whose mother you're sweet on, son?"

Slocum said nothing.

"I don't put ingredients in willy-nilly, you know," Jerrold said. "I need to go back and see what's in the wagon and what I was likely to have added." He frowned. "The color of that last batch was off, wasn't it?"

"Off? What do you mean?"

"It was a mite too brown. I must have put something in to clear up the earlier potion, make it amber, like a good beer."

"What was it? That must be what's needed to help the diphtheria patients!"

"Yup, that must be it. The leaves and all the rest, well, they might not be necessary at all. Or maybe they are, only a pinch of persimmon needs to be added."

"Persimmon? That's it?"

"I call it that because of the smell. I collected the plant around here, though I don't know the name. Big Elk showed me." Jerrold glanced over his shoulder. "He's getting a mite restive. I need to help him finish the ceremony. I can get him to vouch for you. We can spend the night, then—"

"We have to clear out fast," Slocum said.

Jerrold started to ask why, then saw the blood specks on Slocum's shirt. He reached out, pressed a finger into the largest, and it came away sticky with the dead sentry's blood.

"This is going to be a big problem if they find you upped and killed one of their braves." Jerrold stroked his chin whiskers as he thought. "I reckon I better make haste, too. I've been with Big Elk, who will vouch for my whereabouts, but none of 'em will believe I don't know you if they run you down. And they will."

"This is a war party," Slocum said. "What are they going to do?"

"Don't know, don't care. I heard a couple of the braves talking about an army post. I shut out what they were saying."

"You speak Sioux?"

"I learned the lingo years back when one of 'em was at Harvard being shown around like some damned specimen."

"I thought you hadn't really gone to Harvard."

Jerrold snorted and pushed Slocum back into the woods.

"I'll tell Big Elk how I have to mosey on right now. He won't like it, but he's got what he needs from me. The omens were favorable because I gave him all the right chemicals to toss into the fire. The Great Spirit will smile on their attack."

"Getting back to my horse is going to take a while," Slocum said. "I left it on the far side of the camp."

"Don't risk it. Hide in my wagon. If you came in by the road—it's the only one—I'll leave the same way. No choice about that. You hide in the wagon and then drop off when we get close to your horse. From there we'll have to hightail it out of here."

"Going back down that road will leave us sitting ducks."

Jerrold laughed. "That's not how I'd leave. There's a river on the far side of that hill. If we follow it down, it'll put us miles closer to Sentinel Butte, to boot."

The chants died down. Jerrold put his forefinger to his lips, cautioning Slocum to silence, then hurried back to sit beside the medicine man. Slocum waited long enough to assure himself Jerrold wasn't in any danger. Big Elk and the snake oil salesman sat knee-to-knee discussing whatever it was they had to discuss.

Moving softly, Slocum retraced his steps to the wagon. He started to climb in, then considered what might happen if the Indians caught him inside. He worked his way back under the wagon, found dangling chains, and pulled himself up so he hung from the bottom of the wagon bed. It was uncomfortable and would get a sight worse when Jerrold got rolling, but he wasn't as likely to be seen here in the dark.

Barely had he shifted to get more comfortable when he heard Big Elk and Josiah Jerrold returning to the wagon.

Thinking Slocum was hiding there, Jerrold tried to keep the medicine man from entering the wagon. Slocum thanked his lucky stars for his own foresight. Whatever the shaman had wanted to do inside, he did. Slocum heard the creaking boards from two men's footsteps inches above his face, then nothing. Peering toward the rear of the wagon he saw Big Elk's moccasined feet walking away.

"Here we go," Jerrold called out. "Wherever you are, son, hang on tight!"

Even with the warning, the lurch almost dislodged Slocum. He clung tenaciously as the wagon rolled around the camp, found the deep ruts of the road, and settled into them.

"How far's your horse?"

"Close. Another hundred yards," Slocum called out, knowing the clatter of chains and the creaking of harnesses would mask his voice if any of the Sioux were close enough to overhear.

"Better get off now. I hear something from the direction of the camp, and it doesn't sound pleasant."

Slocum heard the shouts, too. He worked his way out of the cradle of dangling straps and chains, hit the ground hard enough to jar him for an instant, then scrambled to his feet and ran to where his mare waited patiently. He vaulted into the saddle and rode to get in front of the wagon so he would be shielded if any of the Indians looked out from their campsite.

"Can't tell for certain sure, but they might have found their sentry," Jerrold called.

"Can you go faster?"

"Have to." Josiah Jerrold snapped the reins and bucked up over the ruts in the road, heading directly across the grassy meadow. "You see that big dark spot ahead? That's where the forest gives way to the river. The banks are rocky but passable, even for my wagon."

"You get on over there," Slocum said. "I'm going to have to decoy them away."

A quick look over his shoulder confirmed Slocum's worst fears. A half dozen braves had mounted and were riding from the camp. He didn't think they were out for an evening constitutional. They had found their dead comrade and were hunting for his killer.

Slocum rode hard, galloping along the twisting road that led back down the mountain. If he was caught, it didn't matter, as long as Jerrold reached Sentinel Butte with his knowledge of what drug might have been omitted from his elixir.

15

Slocum rode as fast as he could but worried that his horse would step in a marmot hole or otherwise stumble in the dark. Without a decent moon to light the way, which wouldn't rise for another couple hours, the darkness was almost complete. Added to this, heavy rain clouds constantly moving across the sky muted even the starlight. He kept his head down although the Indians pursuing did not fire at him.

He wasn't sure what he was going to do. If he tried following the road back down the mountain, he was a goner. Holding the high ground, the Sioux would pick him off as he followed the switchbacks in the trail. Whatever he did, it had to be soon. He saw the broad dirt fan out at the top of the road and knew he had to make a decision fast.

Then Slocum knew he had jumped from the frying pan into the fire. As careful as he had been hiding his trail, Marshal Sully and his posse had tracked him. A half dozen of the lawmen trotted out at the bottom of the trail and spread out, blocking his retreat.

Behind him came the Sioux war party. Ahead was the posse that had dogged him for weeks now. Slocum understood how a horseshoe hot from the forge felt. The hammer came down and smashed him into the anvil. Even as this thought crossed his mind, another replaced it. He slowed his headlong rush. Behind he heard the Indian ponies speeding up. They knew they had him.

When he heard the first war whoop, he drew his six-shooter and began firing at the posse. Slocum knew he couldn't hit anything in the dark, and he didn't want to. He needed as many of the lawmen as possible alive and furious and willing to fight.

The Sioux came closer and fired a few rounds at him. The bullets sailed above him and added to the confusion among the marshal's men.

Slocum veered sharply to the left and hoped he was hidden by the night. For a heart-stopping minute, he thought both the law and the war party were onto his trick. Then the two bands crashed together, the Indians whooping and Marshal Sully shouting out orders to get his men ready for the fight of their lives.

Slocum kept riding until his mare began to falter. He slowed. The sounds of battle came to him from a distance. If it hadn't been for Sully and his single-minded determination, Slocum would never have escaped the Sioux. He took no satisfaction that the Indian war chief fought the federal marshal. Only a soul-blanketing tiredness held him in its grip. He slowed to a walk and let his horse regain her wind. Then he picked up the gait and saw the dark stretch Jerrold had pointed out. He hoped the peddler hadn't steered him wrong as he rode smack into the middle of the shadowy gap.

He yelped when his horse rocked back on its heels and slid down a stretch before recovering. He heard running water and went toward it. Before he came to the river, he saw wagon tracks. Fresh ones. Jerrold had successfully made it this far.

The fact that the medicine wagon was nowhere to be seen heartened Slocum. That meant the going here was easy. And in a few hundred yards the terrain leveled out, the broad riverbanks now dry after the spring runoff had receded. He let his horse make her own way as he strained to hear if anyone pursued.

Even the gunfire had been swallowed by distance. He wondered who had won the skirmish—marshal or war chief. If Sully had gained the upper hand, he would find himself overwhelmed quickly by the rest of the Sioux from the encampment. If the Sioux wiped out the posse, Slocum was safe. They would assume Sully had been responsible for the death of their sentry and not press the matter further. Big Elk might wonder if Jerrold had had a role in the death, but the medicine man was shrewd enough not to say more. Any indictment of Jerrold would also cast him in a bad light.

From what Slocum had seen, the shaman enjoyed a position of power. He wouldn't relinquish that easily. Whatever he told the chief had to be couched in mystical terms. The triumph over the posse would go a long way toward bolstering Big Elk's power.

Slocum overtook Josiah Jerrold before sunrise.

"I left because I didn't want to catch the disease," Jerrold said as he rolled back into Sentinel Butte. "Even if I can find what I did with the earlier formula, I'm afraid I might catch it."

"You haven't so far."

"I've avoided most of the sick bastards," Jerrold said uneasily. "I might say I am a doctor, but I don't do anything but fleece the crowds. I sell cheap whiskey and—"

"And you came upon a way to make it easier for the sick to get better. It might not be a cure, but it gives them time to get better on their own." Slocum had a jaundiced view of doctors. During the war he had seen more deaths in the hospitals than he had on the battlefield, and most of those deaths were caused by the doctors and their barbaric surgery. Better to avoid doctors entirely.

But Jerrold had accidentally found a drug that worked. Slocum didn't care if he actually held a degree from Harvard or lied about it and everything else. Maybe a patient had died and forever soured Jerrold on the profession, or it could have been anything else that made him want to disavow any connection with Harvard Medical School. It didn't matter. His elixir had worked—just a little, but enough.

"That'd make me some kind of hero," Jerrold said glumly. "I don't want to be a hero. That's not who I am."

Slocum had to laugh. He appreciated that sentiment. Heroes had a way of turning out to have feet of clay. Jerrold saw himself as a confidence man, and anything that shook that basic belief had to be wrong.

"Go on, you son of a bitch, laugh if you will. I'm clearing out of here as soon as I can."

Slocum sobered. Josiah Jerrold knew what he wanted to do. Slocum wished he was as sure of his own intentions. His heart jumped a little when he saw Meghan Mallory come from the doctor's office. She brushed back her hair to get it out of her eyes. For an instant the sun caught her just right and turned her into an angel. Then a cloud floated over the sun and changed the aspect to shadow.

But the sun came out again when she saw him and smiled. She waved and called, "You're back. I knew you'd find Dr. Jerrold! You're back!"

"Wish I had a filly as eager to see me," Jerrold said in a low voice. He snapped the reins and brought his wagon into place in Sentinel Butte's main street. With a deft twirl, he looped the reins around the brake and jumped down. Slocum had already dismounted and found himself with an armful of warm, passionate woman.

Slocum kissed her and then gently pushed her away. It

wasn't seemly for a lady to show such affection in public, not that anyone other than Jerrold saw. The tents were filled with even more sick people, and Wilson was nowhere to be seen.

"What's the secret ingredient?" she asked anxiously. "You found him. Did you ask? What is it? Frank needs it so." She swallowed and half turned to look over the rows of tents. "So do the others. Most of the town has come down with the disease. Dr. Wilson is claiming Sentinel Butte might not survive. Even if most of the people recover, they'll leave because of the bad memories."

"What is the ingredient you left out?" Slocum asked Jerrold, who watched them with some amusement.

"Can't say exactly, but it smells like persimmon. I can give you a list of plants to collect. With some experimenting, I ought to find what I left out of the last batch."

"You said it was something that changed the color."

"A clarifying agent, yes, that might well be what I left out of the formula. Let me make a grocery list for you—for you two—to fetch." Jerrold ducked into the office, leaving Slocum and Meghan outside.

"Sometimes I worried I wouldn't see you again, John. I don't want to lose you, too."

"It was something of a chore finding Jerrold," he said. He didn't bother telling her the details. Meghan might not appreciate that he was arrested by a federal marshal or that he had killed an Indian sentry and stirred up a Sioux war party enough to get it back on the warpath.

"You'll have to tell me about it. In detail," she said, moving closer and rubbing against him like an amorous cat. Meghan jerked back when Jerrold returned.

"Here it is. The list of what you need to find. I'll do what I can with the ingredients left in the wagon." Jerrold cleared his throat. "I have some of Big Elk's medicine, too. That might help, though I doubt it. Experimentation is needed."

Jerrold sighed. "I worry that many of the patients won't last long enough to give me results."

"Where can we hunt for these?" Slocum studied the list and saw that Jerrold had sketched what the plants looked like. Without that aid, Slocum would never have known what to collect.

"Back up in the hills above town," Meghan said. "I recognize some of these. We'll have to search for others. It might take a while."

"Get all of them before you return," Jerrold said. He mopped his forehead and then looked sharply at Slocum. "It's the heat, dammit. The heat. I should have stayed in the mountains where it's downright chilly. That's the kind of temperature I prefer." Jerrold went off grumbling to himself about the sultry day.

"Is he all right?" Meghan asked.

Slocum hoped so. Jerrold appeared a shade paler now than he had when they were dodging Indians and posse up in the mountains.

"Time's a-wasting," he said. "You get your horse. I'll make sure we have supplies enough to get what we need on a single trip."

Slocum watched Meghan rush off, admiring the sway of her hips and the fine, firm profile as she turned the corner to go to the stable. He jumped into the medicine wagon and rummaged through the equipment, finding more burlap bags for the plants and taking some of the jerky Jerrold had traded for with the Sioux. Jerked buffalo meat tasted better than anything he had in his saddlebags.

Mounting and riding slowly down the street, Slocum saw that few businesses were open and those that showed any sign of life had their doors closed. People looked out suspiciously as he passed.

Meghan joined him a few blocks down, looking flushed. The shy smile she gave him convinced him she looked forward to being in the hills with him hunting for medicine. Or maybe she just looked forward to being in the hills with him, period.

They didn't say much as they made their way into the foothills and found a steep trail to higher elevations.

"Here's a good place. I think that's a patch of some of the plants Dr. Jerrold wanted."

Slocum took out the list and matched the shape of the leaves. A slow smile came to him.

"We've got most of them here. We can be back fast."

Meghan only nodded. Slocum realized she was as conflicted as he was about this. Collect the medicine fast, less time together. But they had to return the plants if she wanted her son and the others to get better. The diphtheria was taking quite a toll on Sentinel Butte.

They traded few comments as they worked through the afternoon, but as the sun dipped low, Slocum said, "We ought to get back. We've collected almost everything."

"There's still one plant we didn't find," Meghan pointed out. "We have to go up higher, up onto that mesa." She pointed.

"That's a hard ride. We'd have to spend the night there, even if we found the herbs right away."

"We can't go back until we have found everything," Meghan insisted. "What if that one is the essential ingredient?"

Slocum considered all aspects of what she said. Spending the night with her on the mesa was attractive, but there was more, too. She was right about the medicinal plant. If they had to return because they had neglected to find the single one Jerrold needed, another day would be wasted. Better to take a few more hours, then ride back at sunrise.

"Let's go," Slocum said, looking up higher in the hills. The sun was dipping low on the horizon, outlining the distant mountains and giving a touch of chill to the breeze after a hot day.

They rode up a narrow trail and finally emerged on the mesa. From here they had a decent view of Sentinel Butte. Slocum stared at the town, knowing the epidemic that raged there.

"It's hard to believe, isn't it, John? It looks so peaceful down below and it really isn't."

"More peaceful than usual," Slocum said. "I doubt there are many in the saloons whooping it up."

Meghan moved closer and pressed warmly against him. She put her arms around his waist and held him close. He snaked his arm around her shoulders. They didn't have to be this close to share thoughts and needs.

She looked up, but before she could speak Slocum kissed her. She responded immediately, turning in his arms to press hard against him. The kiss lasted for an eternity, an eternity so long the sliver of waxing moon had risen by the time they parted.

"I want you," Slocum said.

Meghan answered by pulling out a blanket and spreading it on the ground. Slocum added his saddle blanket to hers to give them a little padding below their bodies. By the time he had finished smoothing it out he looked up to see that Meghan had stepped out of her clothing and stood naked in the wan silver moonlight. It turned her into an alien creature so heartbreakingly lovely Slocum could hardly stand it. Before he could say anything, she stepped forward and gently pushed him to the blankets.

He settled back and let her unfasten his gunbelt and then work on his jeans. He sighed in relief as she freed his straining erection from its cloth prison. She immediately straddled his waist and settled down. Like a hawk, he watched her every move, marveling at how her skin had turned to such pure marble in the moonlight. But stone never felt so warm and yielding.

Reaching out, he cupped her breasts. She added her hands atop his and pulled them down harder. He felt her heart, her breathing, her vitality. Then he felt even more as she rose, positioned her hips, and settled down again, this time with him fully within her heated interior.

He pushed with his hands and caused her to rise slowly. Then he relaxed and she sank back, taking him fully once more. Meghan twisted slowly from side to side, stirring his fleshy stalk around within her. Then she lifted and dropped again. Slocum abandoned his post on her breasts and got the first spoken response from her.

"No, no, oh!"

He let her breasts swing free because he had switched his grip to her fleshy buttocks. Squeezing, kneading, pulling, and pushing, he guided her to a more energetic movement. Her sighs and moans of pleasure encouraged him to do even more. His finger probed and stroked, poked and pushed and ran over her most sensitive flesh. Every touch pushed her arousal to a higher level. And she never stopped moving.

"I want you so much, John. I do, I do!"

Her hips flew faster now. She leaned forward so she could shove herself downward more forcefully while kissing him. Slocum's hands roved her back, traced over every bone in her spine. He stroked over the back of her head and laced his fingers through her long, midnight-dark hair. All the while they moved together. As Meghan shoved downward, Slocum found himself arching his back to sink even farther into her molten core.

In the warm evening, bathed in silver moonlight, they made love until they were both sated. Meghan shuddered with release, sighed, and then stretched out beside Slocum, clinging to him fiercely.

"I don't want this moment to ever end," she said. "Make love to me again."

He laughed. "You're getting greedy. It'll take a while, but I don't want it to end, either."

"Good."

She snuggled closer. Her gentle hot breath caressed his neck as she rested her face against his shoulder. After a while, Slocum began exploring her delightful body again, and the stirrings he felt were shared.

By the time they were both totally exhausted, having lost themselves in each other, the moon was well past the zenith and sliding downward into the west. All too soon, the rising sun told them they had to finish their search for the herb and return to town.

16

"Something's different," Slocum said as they rode back into Sentinel Butte. He looked around, trying to figure out what it was. He couldn't. The same stillness that had settled over the plague-gripped town continued to make the main street seem more like a cemetery than a vibrant, living place where commerce was conducted. Even the few stores that had been open for business the day before were now closed.

But the eerie silence was different, and Slocum worried about that.

"I don't care," Meghan said. "I just want the doctor to mix up his medicine and give it to Frank. He's gone through so much."

"Does he know about his pa?"

"I think so. He was so sick I never really told him. But he must know because his father's not been at the bedside once."

Slocum considered this and knew the boy had bigger problems with the diphtheria. He had been feverish so long that he probably didn't know where he was, much less that his pa hadn't been to see him.

"You go ahead," Slocum said, reaching over and taking

the leather thong off the hammer of his six-shooter. "I want to prowl around a bit."

"Please, John. You need to give it all to Dr. Jerrold. You've seen him mixing up the elixir and can save time giving him what he needs."

"He knows better than I ever could," Slocum said, distracted. "I never watched him that close."

"John," she said in a voice that he could not refuse. He nodded once, then put his heels to his horse to hurry along. Whenever he felt like he was being watched, he had to see who was spying on him—and that was the sensation he had now. No one showed at any of the windows along the main street. He looked higher, along the roof lines. He stiffened suddenly, thinking he saw the flash of a tall, dark Stetson ducking down atop the three-story hotel. He studied the spot for a moment, then knew he couldn't be sure if he had seen something or had only let his nerves get the better of him.

"Let's make it fast," he said. He trotted to the doctor's office and saw that for the most part nothing had changed. The patients who had been in the tents when he and Meghan had left the day before were still in the same places. But one thing had changed. He dropped to the ground and began working his way down the line of tents. Four of the patients had died and no one had bothered dragging their bodies to the corpse shed.

"Dr. Wilson! Dr. Jerrold!" Meghan jumped to the ground and clutched at the burlap bags filled with the plants they had collected. "We're back!" She went inside the office while Slocum continued to count the living and the dead.

Before he had reached the far end of the tents, Meghan rushed back out, horrified.

"He's dead! Dr. Wilson's dead! And Dr. Jerrold is sick."

Slocum knew what had happened. Wilson died, Jerrold fell, and there'd been no one left to move the bodies of those others who died. No one had been strong enough even to move Wilson's body, apparently, if he was still in his office.

Ducking inside, Slocum took in the grim scene in a single quick glance. Wilson lay slumped over his desk. He had not even stretched out on a pallet. From the blanket on the floor next to Frank Mallory came a weak groan that caught Slocum's attention.

"Son, here. Gotta talk."

Slocum knelt beside Josiah Jerrold.

"You were right. You should have stayed away," Slocum said. "If you know how to mix up your potion, it'll likely save a lot of folks, you included."

"Can't. Too weak. Can't even focus my eyes. I heard you." Jerrold blinked and Slocum saw a milky film over the man's eyes. "You gotta cook up the brew. You know which to use."

"We brought all of them back. You've got to give me some idea." Slocum grabbed the sacks from Meghan and opened them. He held up each plant in turn, waiting for a reaction. "This one?" he said when Jerrold responded to the plant he and Meghan had found on the mesa. "Is this the one missing from the tonic you made up last?"

"You move a muscle, and I swear I'll shoot."

Slocum whirled about, hand going to his six-gun. He froze when he saw that Marshal Sully had the drop on him and his deputy held a six-shooter to Meghan's head. A filthy paw was clamped over the woman's mouth to keep her from calling out a warning.

"There's an epidemic raging. Dr. Jerrold can help. One of these—" Slocum started to grab a burlap bag and Sully fired. The bullet tore through the burlap and knocked a splinter from the floor.

"You fool!" Slocum shouted. "You're going to kill all these people if he doesn't—" A second bullet grazed Slocum's wrist, causing him to recoil involuntarily.

"You drop that hogleg. I'm takin' you to jail till I kin see you in shackles on your way back to Fargo."

"Do what you want, but let Jerrold do his work."

"Looks like you mighta kilt him," the deputy said, looking past Meghan's head. "Don't seem to be stirrin' round none."

"Jerrold!" Slocum moved to shake Jerrold in frustration and was rewarded with the marshal's pistol slamming down hard on the top of his head. Stunned, Slocum dropped to his knees and reached for his head.

Marshal Sully's second blow knocked Slocum flat. He was aware of the marshal snaring his Colt Navy and pulling it out of his holster. Then the red pain turned black, and Slocum passed out.

He groaned and stirred, only to fall heavily to the floor. Slocum shook his head and worried something had broken loose inside. He touched his scalp, and his fingers came away sticky with his own blood. His vision was doubled, but it cleared as he came to realize the marshal had made good on his threat. Slocum was locked up in the town jail.

"Quit makin' so danged much noise," came a querulous voice that Slocum recognized. He forced himself to sit up, his back to the cot he had fallen off. Sully's deputy glared at Slocum from the other side of the steel bars.

"I want to talk to the marshal," Slocum said.

"He ain't available."

"This is important to the likes of you. People are dying all around, if you hadn't noticed. I can save them. Some of them," Slocum amended. "Jerrold needs my help now that the town doctor's dead."

"You mean that pill peddler? He's laid up bad hisse'f," the deputy said.

Slocum sat on the edge of the cot. He'd had the unsettling feeling something was haywire when he rode back into town. The feeling doubled now.

"Why won't you let me talk to the marshal?"

"You shut that piehole of yours," the deputy snapped.

"He was looking poorly when I saw him." Slocum

rubbed the top of his head where the marshal had buffaloed him. Another lump had formed from the second round of pistol strikes. "He's sick, isn't he?"

"Sully's a tough galoot. Don't go pretendin' you care one whit for him."

"I don't, but you might help him if you let me help Dr. Jerrold. More than the marshal can be saved."

"I don't buy it," the deputy said, then laughed. "Git it? I don't *buy* it. Neither your words nor your poison."

Slocum leaned back and looked around. This was a sturdier cell than the one he had broken out of a couple days back. It hardly seemed possible that so much had happened in such a short while. He closed his eyes, remembering the night he had spent with Meghan atop the mesa. The world could have stopped then and there, and it would have been fine with Slocum. But that hadn't happened. Everything moved on, grinding out trouble after trouble, until he wondered how it could ever come to an end short of dying.

"You ever going to feed me?"

"I suppose I ought to, but the restaurant's closed."

"There's a boardinghouse at the edge of town. I rode past it. The landlady's likely to have spare food for a prisoner," Slocum said, wanting the deputy to take as much time as possible, so he could examine the cell more carefully. He had to escape. If the marshal and his sense of justice died, the remaining posse was likely to string up their prisoner and not give it a second thought.

From what Slocum remembered seeing of Marshal Sully, the man wasn't likely to be in any condition to keep his deputies in line.

"You think the landlady'd have more than scraps left over?"

Slocum said nothing. If he sounded too eager, the deputy would never leave. If he looked sullen, the man would take it as a clue he had Slocum securely locked up and never give a thought to him trying to escape.

"I won't be long. Don't go nowhere." The deputy laughed at his little joke and slammed the office door as he left. Slocum stayed where he was, counting slowly. When he got to twenty, the door opened suddenly, letting in a puff of humid night air. The deputy held his six-shooter as if expecting Slocum to have miraculously escaped. He nodded once, holstered his six-shooter, and closed the door again.

This was Slocum's signal to get to work.

He got to his feet and staggered the two paces to the bars. The marshal's clubbing left him dizzy and disoriented, but he had little time to waste. A quick examination of the lock showed that it wouldn't give if he simply tried kicking the door open. He had seen some cells that were so old and rusted such a trick would work. The only thing preventing it then was the presence of a marshal or a deputy keeping a sharp eye out for such an escape attempt.

The hinges in this jail were similarly in good condition. The hinge pins had caps secured over the top and bottom to prevent him from knocking them out and pushing the door open that way. Slocum worked faster, feeling the crush of time on him. The other cell had given him rotted wood as an escape path. The Sentinel Butte jail cell was too well maintained for that. The bolts holding the cell to the wall were sturdy, and the wall was masonry. He might chip his way out if he had a hammer and chisel and plenty of time. He didn't have any of those.

A quick examination of the high, small barred window convinced him escape was impossible that way. Even with the bars removed, he wasn't sure he could squeeze through the remaining hole. He turned his attention to the floor. He pried up a board and found only hard-packed dirt. Given time he could tunnel out—given a week, that is. He dropped the board back into place when he heard boot steps outside the jail.

The deputy had returned with a tray of food.

"Got you some grub, Slocum. It's too danged good for the likes of you, if you ask me, but it's what the marshal would want. You step on back away from the door."

The deputy put the tray on the floor, got out a large key, and turned it in the lock. Before he opened the door, he drew his pistol. As the cell door opened, he pushed the tray in with his toe until he could close and lock the door again. Only then did he relax.

He was too good at guarding his prisoner for Slocum's liking.

But the food was what he needed. The plate of beef stew was about the best he had ever tasted, even if the meat was tougher than shoe leather and the vegetables were blanched a uniform pasty white. It had been too long since he had eaten a hot meal to complain. The cornbread with the stew went down fine, too.

Slocum turned the tray sideways and put it through the bars onto the floor outside the cell but the bowl wouldn't fit.

"What do you want me to do with this?"

"Hell, lick it clean for all I care. I ain't riskin' an escape."

"The landlady'd want her bowl and spoon back." Slocum held up the shiny spoon. If he could keep the spoon, he had another possible way to get out. Using the handle in the lock, he might force the tumblers enough to open the door.

Slocum kept from whopping with glee when the deputy told him to shut up and go back to sleep.

Pretending to obey, Slocum lay on the cot, watching the deputy through half-closed lids. As he expected, the deputy propped his feet up on the desk, tilted his hat down, and was softly snoring within minutes. Slocum waited a while longer before silently going to the cell door and shoving the spoon handle into the lock. As he moved it up and down trying to open the tumblers, tiny scraping sounds echoed louder than gunshots to Slocum's ears, but the deputy never stirred.

Emboldened, Slocum worked harder to jimmy the lock. He had to twist his wrist in an awkward direction, but this had come down to being his only way to escape. The cell was too securely constructed for any other way out.

Sweat poured down Slocum's face, but he kept working, letting it burn his eyes. Taking even a second to wipe it off his face would take away from the time he needed to pick the lock.

When his wrist felt as if he had broken it, Slocum pulled out the spoon and crept back to the cot. He rubbed his hand and forearm to get the strained muscles loosened up again, but he hadn't budged the lock. It was too secure for his meager attempts at jailbreaking.

He lay down but did not sleep. He watched the deputy and considered other ways of luring him to the door. The spoon handle had been worn down to a sharp point. If he could grab the deputy and pull him close, he could use it as a knife.

Then Slocum saw that the deputy had hung the cell door keys on a hook. If he came to investigate and Slocum successfully grabbed and threatened him, it would be for naught if the keys were still across the room.

"His gun," Slocum said softly to himself. "I grab his gun and shoot the son of a bitch if he doesn't let me out." That plan was taking shape when Slocum saw the jail office door open a few inches. He noticed only because of the breeze that came through the door an instant before Meghan Mallory.

She put her finger to her lips to keep him quiet.

Slocum waved her off, not wanting her to get involved. The posse had captured their road agent and wouldn't take kindly to anyone aiding and abetting his escape. Slocum got to his feet and started to call out to her so the deputy would wake up. Letting her get tossed into the cell, too, was out of the question. She had a sick boy to look after and could hardly do that from inside the jail.

But before so much as a word could form on his lips, Slocum watched Meghan bring her hand out from the folds of her skirt. She held a large rock. She lifted it and brought it down smartly on the top of the deputy's head. The man grunted, uncrossed his arms, and then fell out of the chair. He laid facedown on the floor as a tiny trickle of blood oozed from the cut on his scalp.

"Hurry, John," Meghan said. She grabbed the key ring and tossed it to him. She rummaged through the desk and found his Colt Navy and knife. By the time he was free of the cell, she was ready to hand them to him.

He kissed her, but she shied away.

"There's not enough time," she said. "The rest of the posse has been patrolling the town, shooting looters. I never thought I'd hate to see men upholding the law, but they are relentless."

"The marshal taught them too well," Slocum said. He strapped on his gun and tucked his knife away in his boot.

"Is it true? That they arrested you for robbing a stagecoach?"

"I never robbed that stage," Slocum said truthfully. "They laid a trap and I sprung it."

"That's a relief. I didn't want to believe them when they said you were this desperado who—" She cut off her words, then smiled strangely. "Well, I *know* you're a desperado. That's exactly what I need most now."

"How's Jerrold doing?"

She shook her head. "Not too well. He's delirious and nothing he says makes any sense. It's as if he is trying to mix up the right drugs but is too far gone in a fever dream to do it."

"I'll try to figure out how he made the potion that worked," Slocum said. "The most I ever mixed together before was beans and bacon, but I have to try."

"No," Meghan said, grabbing his arm. "You've got to get

out of town. The posse isn't going to take kindly to you escaping."

"The marshal's laid up, too, isn't he?"

"He's sick but not delirious. He would order his men to shoot you on sight. He's as rigid an upholder of the law as any man I've seen," she said.

Slocum dragged the unconscious deputy into the jail cell and locked the door. He threw the keys onto the desk well out of the man's reach.

"He'll call out for help. The others will hear him," Meghan said dubiously.

"What do you want me to do, kill him?"

"I . . . I don't know. I want to do whatever it'll take to save my son." She clutched him tightly and confessed, "If I thought you killing him would do a damned thing to save Frank, I'd take the six-shooter and do it myself."

Gunfire outside set Slocum into motion. He spun Meghan around to get her out of the line of fire, then opened the jail door a fraction to peer out. The posse had cornered a pair of looters who'd chosen to shoot it out rather than hightail it.

"Go, John. This is your chance while they're busy. Get out of town now and save yourself."

He looked into her bright, teary eyes, kissed her, and then slipped through the door into the night. Going down side streets and hiding in alleyways got him to the livery stable undetected. He saddled his mare and rode from town, going south because he knew what trouble lay to the west and the east.

17

The sun rose on Slocum's left shoulder and gave a hint as to how stifling the day would be. The sky lacked clouds, except for a white fringe on the far horizon, and somehow the sun had boiled up arrogant and all full of itself after only scant minutes. Slocum stared at the terrain ahead. The prairie flattened out here, getting away from the hills surrounding Sentinel Butte. As he rode, he thought of how he had spent such delightful time in those hills with Meghan, on the mesa looking down at the silent town, hunting for the medicinal plants needed to preserve the flickering life in the diphtheria victims.

He thought on it all, and he slowed. His horse nickered, then turned sharply eastward into the sun. Slocum let the horse have its head and soon found a pool of water. What fed the pond he couldn't say, since it hadn't rained in days. While the horse drank, Slocum splashed water on his face. The feel of the cleansing moisture let him think more clearly.

He was running away, pure and simple. It wasn't anything he hadn't done before. More than once he had stayed a step ahead of the law by clearing out of a town. While he didn't think of himself as an outlaw, he'd had more than his share of run-ins with men wearing a badge. Marshal Sully's trap back in Fargo had been sprung before he could rob the stage, but if he hadn't fallen into the ambush, he would have stolen the shipment and never thought twice about the theft.

But now a knot of worry grew and festered in him. Running away now was wrong. People other than Meghan Mallory and her son needed him back in Sentinel Butte, and he was abandoning them. Some had already died. Dr. Wilson would neither know nor care if Slocum kept riding, but Josiah Jerrold was alive. Or he had been.

In his mind Slocum saw the man reaching up to him from his bed on the thin blanket, shaky hand outstretched, feverish eyes not seeing but still imploring. Jerrold thought he knew the secret ingredient to the tonic and could fix it. What that secret might be, John Slocum didn't know. He splashed more water on his face and tried to remember if he had watched Jerrold concocting his elixir.

He had, but the man hadn't given Slocum any hint what he did. Slocum had watched and seen—and couldn't tell what Jerrold had done to make his original potion.

"Except . . ." Slocum said. His mare looked over at him, then went back to drinking. He would have to stop her soon to keep her from bloating. Slocum shoved his entire head under the water and came up sputtering.

Except rang in his head like a bell. Of all the people in the world, he was the only one who might find what Josiah Jerrold had done.

"Come on," Slocum said, tugging at the horse's reins. Reluctantly, the mare stopped drinking and let Slocum mount. When he wheeled about to head north, the horse turned a big brown inquiring eye up at him. The mare whinnied until Slocum patted her neck and reassured her he knew what he was doing.

Or he thought he knew what he was doing. He headed back to Sentinel Butte.

*   *   *

"You'll get yourself killed, John, and for what?" Meghan protested on his return. She sat on a milking stool beside her son. Frank's complexion had turned pasty white again, and the fever burned at his brain. The boy never even opened his eyes as his mother spoke. "You shouldn't have returned."

"He's still alive," Slocum said, looking over at Jerrold, "but for how much longer?"

"How long will any of them live?" Meghan asked. "Some get better, but most are dying."

"The ones that survive, are they helping?"

She shook her head sadly. "Most want only to leave town. A few loaded their families into wagons and left, fearing their kin would catch the disease, too."

"If they avoided it this long, chances are good they won't get it at all," Slocum said.

"You look a little peaked," Meghan said. "You're not coming down with it, are you?"

Slocum tried to get his thoughts into order to answer properly. Everything was jumbled up and had been since he had decided to return.

"I haven't slept since the marshal laid me out with his gun barrel," Slocum said. "Haven't eaten, either."

"So what do you think you can do?"

"Jerrold must have left notes, or given a hint by what he had out on his workbench, something. I saw him mixing up the elixir he sold originally and know what he said about the real drug acting to turn the liquid a clear amber. I remember how it looked. If I can mix his chemicals until I get something that looks right, I might save a lot of these people."

"You'll get yourself strung up. That deputy Leroy was spitting mad," Meghan said. "I almost confessed just to quiet him down. He got red in the face and cursed and began shooting his six-gun at anything that moved. Never have I seen a man so downright angry."

"Keep the cold compresses on their foreheads," Slocum said. "I'm going to sneak into the wagon and do some mixing." He rummaged about the office until he'd collected a few of the empty elixir bottles. As he hunted, he was keenly aware of how Meghan watched him. She had rescued him from the jail cell, only to have him throw away her heroism in what might be a foolish attempt to duplicate a formula the creator didn't even know.

With an armful of the empty bottles, Slocum went to the door and looked out. Sentinel Butte had truly turned into a ghost town. He couldn't know for sure, but half of everyone here might well have died. The undertaker had given up trying to collect all the bodies and refused to budge from his funeral parlor. As soon as Slocum figured out Jerrold's secret ingredients, he vowed to empty the shed filled with corpses. It wouldn't be long before diphtheria was the least of the town's worries. The disease caused by so many decaying bodies would spread death quicker than a prairie fire.

Juggling the bottles, clanking as he went, Slocum reached the medicine wagon and pushed his load inside. He quickly followed the bottles into the close heat of the wagon's interior. Sweat didn't pop out on his forehead now, it exploded. He took off his bandanna and tied it around his forehead like an Apache brave, to stem the river of sweat pouring into his eyes. Even then, his vision was blurry as he sat on the low stool and began pulling down the glass vials of Jerrold's chemical hoard.

He didn't have any idea how to start.

Slocum sat for a full minute, trying to recollect the sequence Jerrold had followed. Working from his spotty memory, he started mixing things together in about the proportions he remembered. More than once he took a big swig from the whiskey bottle that had formed the basis for the potion's usefulness—or so he had thought at the time.

The syrupy look soon matched that of the second batch,

the one that had not worked. Taking out the plants he and
Meghan had just collected, Slocum split his basic solution
into smaller bottles and started adding pinches of each
plant. When he had gone through all the varieties he had
brought back, nothing happened that he could see.

He chewed on his lower lip, then decided to begin adding a second plant to each bottle. His head spun when he
tried to figure out how many combinations this might require him to try. Even if he got one that looked right, that
didn't mean that it was right.

He had pulled out another handful of plants and spread
them on the workbench when a shaft of light from the curtain illuminated the entire interior.

"Close that," he said, irritated. "Meghan?"

"That's 'bout what I thought. It was the bitch what
sprung you from the cell, wasn't it? It'll go easier on you if
you incriminate her."

Slocum grabbed for his six-shooter and then froze. The
double-barreled shotgun pointed directly at him would blast
him into bloody chunks before he could clear leather.

"Dang, I hoped you'da tried to throw down on me. I
want to see a noose round your filthy neck, Slocum. You
made me look like a fool, and after I went and brung you
food."

"It was good stew," Slocum said. He played for time so
he could find a way out of this predicament, but there
wasn't any way short of getting two barrels of double-aught
buck run through his body.

"You git yer ass on outta there. I'm puttin' you back into
that cell." The deputy stepped to one side but held the black
curtain back with the shotgun. "Now."

"I saw the marshal. He's in a bad way."

"Don't you go talkin' bad about Sully. He's tough. He's
gonna make it."

"Not likely, unless I find the right combination to make a
drug that worked before," Slocum said. His lips had turned

gummy and his tongue tried to stick to the roof of his mouth. The world spun around him just a little.

"You ain't makin' me think you kin do what the town doc couldn't. Even that charlatan Jerrold's more likely to whip up the right medicine."

"I traveled with him. I saw him making the potion that worked."

"I told you to git outta there! If I say it again, my request will be accompanied by a shotgun shell full of buckshot."

Slocum pushed his experiment into the center of the workbench so he wouldn't spill any of it. He had to remember what he had already tried and what needed doing. But when he would be allowed to return to his medicine-making was a poser. He stepped out into the bright summer sun and felt as if he had been hit by a huge burning fist.

"Over to the jail. Double time, march!" The deputy prodded him with the shotgun. As Slocum turned, Leroy deftly plucked his six-shooter from its holster.

"Wait!"

The deputy halted and Slocum considered trying to run. Leroy was too alert for that, moving so he could get both Slocum and Meghan into his line of fire.

"I oughta throw you in the clink, too, missy. I know what you done. You helped a known criminal escape my custody."

"You have to let him keep working on the medicine. The marshal needs it. My *son* needs it!" A touch of hysteria came to the woman's voice. The deputy was oblivious to it.

"Move it along. I ain't got all day," Leroy said. Then he laughed. "But you're gonna have all the time in the world 'cuz you're gonna be locked up for a lotta years."

"Please," Meghan said, grabbing the deputy's arm. The lawman jerked free and swung the shotgun around to cover her. Slocum moved like a striking snake, grabbed the barrel, and knocked it up as the deputy pulled the triggers. The recoil knocked Leroy backward. He caught a heel on a rock and fell heavily to land on his ass.

"I'll—" He fumbled for his six-shooter but saw that Slocum wasn't making a move to stop him. The deputy paused, then frowned.

"The marshal," Meghan pleaded. "He can help your marshal."

"I owe Sully my life," Leroy said. "More'n once, actually. When them Injuns attacked us up on the mountain, he saved my hide. Before that, too."

Slocum kept quiet. If the deputy learned how that fight had been started, there was no way in hell Slocum could stay out of a jail cell.

"He can only try. He's the only one who can do even that much," Meghan said.

"Let's go see if the marshal's conscious," the deputy said. He drew his six-gun and pointed it at Slocum. "Don't go tryin' nuthin' funny now, you hear?"

Slocum followed Meghan into the doctor's office. He noticed right away that there was one fewer patient. Trying to figure out who had died was a fool's game he didn't want to play. Frank Mallory moaned softly, Josiah Jerrold lay like the dead, and Marshal Sully was half-propped up in one corner of the room. He weakly motioned for them to come closer.

"You brought 'im. Good. I was afeared he'd run off."

"You wanted me to fetch Slocum here, Marshal?" Leroy looked at Sully as if he had gone around the bend.

"I drift in and out, but I ain't dead yet," Sully said. "I heard what they was sayin' and I believe 'em. Slocum here's most likely to fix up a batch of the doc's medicine. Ain't that right, Slocum?"

"I was trying when he stopped me." Slocum looked at the deputy, who turned suddenly shy. He lowered his six-shooter and looked like a misbehaving child about to be punished.

"I need . . . I need somethin'," the marshal said. "Gettin' hard to think again."

"He's burning up with fever. Well, are you going to allow Mr. Slocum to work or are you going to put him in a cell so your friend can die?" Meghan pursed her lips and glared at Leroy.

"Git on back to work, Slocum. You heard what Sully said." The deputy turned from side to side like a bull in a chute, not knowing what to do next. Meghan remedied that by sending him out to fetch more water for her compresses. She favored Slocum with a quick smile that faded when her son moaned.

Slocum left what was turning into another mortuary and climbed into the wagon. His legs failed him for a moment as he stepped up on the rear stage, but overall he felt stronger, and he plunged into the dark interior and stared at the bottles filled with the basic formula. It took a minute for him to recollect what he had been doing when the deputy interrupted him, but when he started again, the work went quicker.

A pinch here, a bit more, and then moving on to the next bottle. He worked for hours, then leaned back, too tired to continue. None of the fluids matched his visual memory of what Josiah Jerrold had sold originally.

His hands shook as he started to mix another batch of what he thought was the basic formula, then he stopped and stared. Looking closer at one bottle, he grabbed it, held it up to the light coming in from outside, and gently shook it so the liquid sloshed around. Exhaustion suddenly gone, Slocum went to the curtain and pushed it back so he could look at the concoction in the sun. He sank down to the edge of the rear platform and just stared at the bottle in his hand.

"What you got, Slocum? That it? That what the marshal wanted you to find?"

"I think it might be," Slocum said. His mouth was filled

with cotton. He put the bottle to his lips and took a small taste. "It tastes about the same as the other."

"Good?"

"Terrible," he corrected. "But the same." He took another draft, then licked his lips of the drops that escaped his tongue. "This might be it."

"Then give it to me. I'll see that the marshal gits it."

"My son gets it first," Meghan said.

"The marshal. He . . ." The deputy grabbed for Slocum's six-shooter, which he had thrust into his belt, but it was gone. Meghan held it trained on the deputy.

"Go on, John. Give Frank a taste. Then Dr. Jerrold and the marshal."

As he went into the doctor's office, Slocum sampled the medicine one more time, searching his memory for the aftertaste and the bite. His tongue tried to turn somersaults, then tie itself into a granny knot. Slocum made a face. This was as close as he could get.

He administered a tablespoon to Frank Mallory, then to Jerrold and finally to the marshal. The lawman's eyelids fluttered open and he smiled.

"That the stuff?"

"We'll see." Slocum's heart pounded. He poured a spoonful for the lawman and gave it to him.

"If you're not poisonin' me, then that's got to do the trick. It'd take a healthy man to survive such a foul-tastin' potable. Not even the tarantula juice in Maggie Mine's Saloon is this bad."

Slocum had no idea where that saloon was and didn't ask. He watched the marshal closely. There didn't seem to be any change, but the moans from Josiah Jerrold caused him to whirl around. The snake oil salesman propped himself up on one elbow and motioned for Slocum to come closer.

"That's it, son. You done it," Jerrold said. "I'm not up to whipping my weight in wildcats, but I feel it workin' inside me."

"You want more?"

"Only a bit now and then. Share it with the others. The boy?" Jerrold tried to look at Meghan's son, but his strength wasn't up to the chore.

"Gave him some already," Slocum said. "How much should everyone get?"

"Damned if I know. Experiment. That's how you made this, isn't it?" So much effort tuckered out Jerrold, and he sank back to the pallet. His eyes closed, but a small contented smile curled his lips.

"He's breathing easier," Meghan said.

Slocum stared at Josiah Jerrold and couldn't see any difference.

"Frank, he's breathing easier."

"Oh, yeah," Slocum said. He was a mite disoriented.

"Let me dispense the medicine to others," Meghan said, taking the bottle from Slocum's hand.

He tried to tell her something but was unable to remember what it was.

"You rest, John. You've worn yourself to a frazzle."

"Sleep," he said, knowing this was a good idea. He curled up on one of the pallets that had been occupied by another patient, now gone. He hadn't slept in how many hours? He hadn't drunk anything, either, not after his horse at the pond. Food was a distant memory. But he fell asleep with the taste of the medicine on his lips and a warm feeling that he had saved everyone in Sentinel Butte.

18

"He's dying, John, he's dying!"

Slocum stirred. He had been in the middle of a nice dream, and the feel of fingers gripping his shoulder with fierce intensity and shaking him destroyed the mood entirely. He groaned, tried to pull away, and couldn't. Someone began shaking him hard enough to rattle his teeth.

"He's fading fast. You've got to help him. All of them!"

Slocum finally got his eyes open. The blurriness left quickly when he saw Meghan above him.

"What's wrong?"

"Dr. Jerrold, he's gotten worse, a lot worse."

"Give him more of the potion."

"I can't." Tears ran down Meghan's cheeks. "There isn't any more. I . . . I gave the last to Frank."

"What about the rest?"

"Some are better, some are worse," she said. Her panic had faded to a listlessness that worried Slocum more than the fear. He sat up. She hugged him close and sobbed. "The marshal's no better, either."

"But Frank's doing well?"

"I gave him the last of the medicine. He'll need more. They all will."

"The last?" Slocum took a few seconds to figure out that she had run through all the medicine he had fixed. "I can do more."

"Please, John. Do it now. Hurry."

He pried her loose and sat up. He was a little woozy from being awakened this way. He could think of other ways he would prefer Meghan to wake him in the morning. Those thoughts evaporated as he saw that she wasn't exaggerating. Josiah Jerrold lay limp as a rag doll on his bed across the room. His breathing was hurried and shallow, and there was no color at all in his face. Slocum stood, braced himself when he experienced a moment's dizziness, and then looked at Frank Mallory. Meghan's son shivered with fever in spite of the hot day and the blanket over his thin shoulders. The only patient in the room who appeared to be recovering was Marshal Sully. The man slept heavily, his chest rising and falling like a bellows. He snored and twitched, but his color was good.

Slocum looked back at Jerrold and shook his head. The old snake oil peddler might not make it, in spite of the medicine. The potion was no panacea. All it did was hold off diphtheria's symptoms, giving the body time to recover.

Slocum took a few tentative steps, and then forced himself to a surer stride. He stepped into the hot sun and almost passed out. The humidity was stifling, and the heat had magnified from even the day before. He wiped at sweat beading on his forehead and shivered just a little.

"Hurry, John. I don't know how long he has."

Slocum went to the medicine wagon and climbed in. He sat at the workbench and stared at what he had already done. There was plenty of the basic formula, but none of the plant he had used to change the color. Slocum searched through the burlap bags for more and found none. He leaned back and heaved a deep sigh.

He had to go harvest more.

Knowing there wasn't any time to waste, Slocum swung

around and left the wagon. He was a little disoriented out in the sun, but he finally got his bearings and headed for the stable. The necessary plant had been the one from the mesa. Slocum tried to remember how much he and Meghan had collected and felt a moment of despair. To fill a single burlap bag they had picked every single last plant they had found. He needed another patch for a new harvesting.

He saddled his horse and led her from the stable. Meghan stood outside waiting for him.

"It'll go faster with two of us," she said.

"I need more of the plant from the mesa."

She nodded sadly. "I thought so. It was the rarest of the lot we found."

"Who's looking after your boy?"

"A few . . . ladies," she said uneasily.

"Ladies? Do you mean soiled doves?"

"They have been taking care of others felled by the epidemic in their . . . house."

"Brothel."

"Yes, dammit, the whores have been looking after the sick in their brothel," she said angrily. "And I don't care."

"They're human beings, too. What they do for a living doesn't mean they can't care," Slocum pointed out.

"It's not the way I was raised to think of them. So many of the good people in town refused to do anything to help their neighbors for fear of catching the diphtheria that I thought everyone would react the same way."

"It's good they'll take care of Frank," Slocum said. "It'll give us time to locate even more of the plant. You have any idea what it's called? I know snakeweed and blue grama and other grasses, but not this."

"I'm not an expert, and Dr. Jerrold never put a name to it."

"Doesn't matter," Slocum said. He closed his eyes for a moment and let the weariness wash over him. He could have slept for another few hours, but there was no rest for the wicked. Finding the plant and brewing up more of the medicine was some retribution for all the wrongs he had done.

They rode in silence much of the day, each lost in thought. Slocum's mind wandered considerably, and he found it difficult to focus for longer than a few minutes at a time. He found himself relying on Meghan to keep them on the trail leading to the mesa, because he had too much trouble locating landmarks. Even when he did, he couldn't remember where to go after finding them.

They rode onto the mesa in late afternoon. Slocum quickly found the spot where they had picked the plant before. A touch of memory assailed him. He and Meghan had spent a delightful night here. They should have spent the night and then taken the next day to find even more of the medicinal herb.

He hadn't known.

"John, is the sun getting to you?"

"I'm all right," he said. He forced himself to focus on finding another patch of the plants. The original location had been only a small circular area, and nowhere nearby did he see more. "You ride that way, and I'll go this. Shout if you find more."

"You don't look good," she said.

"Go, go." Slocum put his heels to his mare's flanks and trotted off, hunting for terrain that looked like that where they had already gathered. He found a likely area and began a spiral search, slowly widening the circle so he could be sure he didn't miss a single square inch. He found nothing, so he rode farther toward the center of the mesa.

An hour later, he drew rein and simply stared. Then he dismounted and dropped to his knees, plucking at the plants and holding them up to be sure he had indeed found the mother lode.

"Meghan!" he shouted. "Meghan! I found more!"

He stood and looked around for her. Nothing. Slocum

drew his six-shooter and fired it into the air to draw her attention. He hadn't thought they were so far apart she wouldn't hear him call for her—or he wouldn't hear her call for him.

Listening hard, he heard a distant horse neighing. Slocum went cold inside when he realized it wasn't a horse he heard. It was horses. They weren't alone on the mesa. He swung into the saddle and made sure his Colt Navy rode easy as he turned toward the sound of hoofbeats approaching. Meeting the other riders head-on wasn't a smart thing to do when he didn't know who they were, but he had no choice. There was scant place to hide on the mesa, other than ravines cut by rain and wind. He rode in the direction of the riders and instantly regretted it.

The Sioux war party saw him an instant before he spotted them. The whoops and shouts as they galloped for him told of their intent. Slocum wheeled about and raced off, knowing he would never be able to escape the warriors unless they tired and gave up.

He galloped past the patch of herbs he had intended to pick and headed back in the direction he had come, only to see Meghan ahead.

"Indians! Ride!"

Meghan started to question him and then saw his pursuers. She galloped alongside him until both their horses began to flag. Slocum pointed to a deep ravine. She nodded and led the way. They got their horses down into the gully.

"We can't ride that way," she said, pointing.

Slocum saw that she was right. The gully cut through the edge of the mesa and spilled out into empty space. It would have been a spectacular waterfall during a heavy rain, but now it meant they could only sneak in one direction. He took the lead, picking through the large rocks until he began to wonder what had happened to the Sioux braves.

"John, my horse is tuckered out. I am, too."

Slocum drew rein and looked anxiously at the lip of the

ravine a few feet above his head. They were dead ducks if the Indians found them here, but there hadn't been any choice. Trying to make their way back down the winding trail leading to the mesa top would have been suicidal.

"I don't hear them. Did they give up?"

Slocum shook his head. He couldn't figure out why the Indians would give up pursuit so quickly.

"I'm not sure what they're looking for up here. There can't be very good hunting compared to the forests where Jerrold met with Big Elk."

"Big Elk?"

Slocum related the story of the Sioux medicine man, and an idea began to form in his mind. When he finished telling Meghan what had happened before, he said, "That was a small party. Not more than three or four braves."

"So?"

"It's a scouting party, not a war party. They're looking for something, and I think I know what it is."

"What can it be? They wouldn't get close to Sentinel Butte unless it was important."

"It is—to Big Elk." Slocum handed her his horse's reins, climbed up in the saddle, and balanced precariously for a moment so he could look out over the arroyo rim. He got his feet under him the best he could, then jumped, clawing for a root dangling down. It gave way, but he kept scrambling and got to the flat ground above.

"You can't leave me here, John. I don't know what to do!"

"I won't be long." Slocum didn't listen to her protests. His head felt as if it might explode, and he noticed every ache in his body now that he wasn't mounted and riding. Keeping low, he walked toward a spot where he could spy on the Indians' back trail. He flopped on his belly and watched as the three who had chased him and another Sioux stood in a circle some distance off.

The one Indian dropped from his horse and bent over. The distance was too great for Slocum to directly see what happened, but he knew. That was Big Elk and the braves with him had protected the patch of herbs Slocum had meant to pick. The Sioux medicine man harvested the medicinal plants necessary to keep Jerrold, Marshal Sully, Frank Mallory, and others alive.

Slocum faded away and rejoined an anxious Meghan. He told her what he had seen.

"I didn't find any of the plants," Meghan said. "Those might be all that grow up here. We need them! John, my son! Frank will die without the medicine!"

"Calm down," he said. "I need to think." Slocum found this easier to say than do with a headache so bad it felt as if his eyes would explode out the front of his face. Slowly, he worked through the problem and came up with the only possible solution. He looked up at Meghan.

"How can we do that?" she asked. She had reached the same conclusion he had, only a lot faster.

"Like thieves in the night," he said. "That's the only thing we can do. We steal Big Elk's medicine plant from him."

She protested and cried and then raged about how long it would take to find another patch of the proper plant. Slocum let her work out all her fears. He was too exhausted to do more than nod occasionally. When she had run down and her arguments had become repetitious, he said, "You don't have to do anything but get ready to run. I'll steal Big Elk's medicine."

"You're good at that, aren't you?"

"What do you mean?"

"The marshal set a trap for you and you weren't an innocent who happened to stumble into it. You did try to rob the stagecoach."

Slocum didn't bother answering. Meghan already knew the answer. He pulled his hat low to protect his eyes from what little sunlight sneaked over the far rim of the arroyo and settled down to wait for night. The Sioux might not expect nocturnal visitors and would have built a campfire he could use to find them

All he wanted to do was rest his eyes. He came awake when Meghan shook him hard. His hand flashed to his six-shooter, but he didn't draw.

"It's almost midnight. When are you going to steal the plants from them?"

"Midnight?" Slocum fumbled his pocket watch out, opened it, and peered at the face. Meghan was right. He hadn't intended to sleep so long, and he certainly didn't feel rested, even after more than six hours asleep.

"I can smell their campfire," Meghan said. "Not as much as I did when they fixed supper. I haven't picked up anything more than a whiff of burning wood for a couple hours."

"I'd've waited till now anyway," Slocum said. "I want them to be asleep and sure no one is likely to sneak up on them."

"They saw you earlier."

"Let's hope they think they ran me off. Not running me into the ground tells me they had orders to protect Big Elk."

Slocum got his rope from his saddle, lassoed an overhanging tree limb, and walked up the crumbling side of the ravine. He swung onto level ground, got his bearings, and headed for the Sioux encampment. Out of the arroyo he caught the fragrant scent of burning pine. He used this to guide him through the night. By the time he reached a spot only a dozen yards from the well-picked patch of plants he had intended for his own, the sliver of moon had risen, letting him see the ghostly silhouettes of the Sioux asleep in their blankets.

He dropped low and lay watching for what seemed an eternity. The Indians were all soundly asleep and hadn't posted a sentry. Like a snake slithering forward, Slocum made his way closer. The three braves slept away from the fourth dark lump. Slocum knew this had to be Big Elk. When he was within a few feet of the Sioux medicine man, he froze.

Big Elk stirred, muttering to himself and rolling over so he faced Slocum. Slocum watched the shaman's eyes open. He knelt with his hand on the butt of his six-gun but did not draw. The fight would be ferocious if the three braves awoke and found that Slocum had shot their medicine man. And with his pulse hammering in his head like a locomotive piston, Slocum wasn't sure how much of a fight he could put up.

The medicine man closed his eyes and his breathing once more turned regular and slow. He slept.

Slocum worked closer until he found three packs Big Elk had placed at his feet. He knew he couldn't steal all three, because of the rustling sounds caused as he picked up the first bag. Slocum opened it and peered inside. In the darkness he couldn't tell what he had. For all he knew, Big Elk might have collected a wide variety of plants. Reaching in, he pulled out a handful and held the leaves up.

A slow smile crossed his lips. This was what he needed. Slocum hastily checked the other two bags and found them stuffed with the same plant.

He could use all three. Sentinel Butte had plenty of people needing succor from the diphtheria that held them in its deadly grip, but Slocum left one bag and carefully picked up only the other two. The Sioux might need the medicine plant for those of their tribe also caught up in the epidemic.

Slocum began moving slowly away, dragging the two bags. He froze when he heard a Sioux brave call out something in his own tongue.

Big Elk stirred and sat up, facing the others in the camp. Slocum held stock-still as the medicine man replied to whatever the brave had asked of him. Slocum tensed when Big Elk turned a bit more so he could see where he had left the bags at his feet. If he noticed two-thirds of his stash missing, he would sound an alarm. Slocum reached down, fingers curling around the horn handle of his knife.

It took all his self-control not to let out a whoop of glee when Big Elk sank down to his blanket, grumbled a little, and then settled back to sleep. Slocum turned his attention from the medicine man to the brave a few yards away. Every second he remained in the Indian camp he was in danger.

The Sioux warrior did not return to his slumber. He stood and paced around the camp, muttering to himself. Slocum dared not move. This would draw the brave's attention in a flash, yet he could not stay in the camp much longer. It was as if all his strength had drained from his body. Remaining even a minute longer might leave him helpless.

He couldn't move. He couldn't stay.

Slocum lay still for a moment, clinging to the two bags filled with the medicine needed to save everyone in Sentinel Butte. It would save Josiah Jerrold and Marshal Sully . . . and Frank Mallory.

This thought fixed in his head got Slocum moving away inch by inch. He dragged the bags under him as he crept on hands and knees. If the brave spotted him, he might mistake him for a coyote.

Slocum almost laughed aloud. That could be worse than being recognized as a thieving White Eyes.

He felt dizzy and weak and driven. He moved faster, getting away from the Sioux camp. He lifted his head and got his bearings by the stars, then headed for the ravine where he had left Meghan and his horse.

The dark drop-off lay ahead. Slocum doggedly crawled forward, though he was probably out of sight of the Sioux warriors. Somehow, standing wasn't something he wanted to try. His legs worked fine if he crawled. He wasn't sure he could walk without falling over.

Dizzy and aching, he worked his way closer to the edge of the ravine.

"Meghan," he whispered. "Are you there? I have the herbs. Meghan?"

He crawled forward another foot and then fell headlong into the arroyo. Slocum smashed hard into the ground, tried to call out to the woman again, and then could not fight anymore. He passed out.

19

Slocum curled up into a tight ball, freezing to death. His head threatened to explode like a rotted melon hit by a rifle bullet, and it was this that forced him to open his eyes.

"Meghan?" he called out weakly, struggling even to breathe. He straightened and found that he was still clinging to the bags of medicinal leaves stolen from Big Elk. Weird thoughts fluttered through his head. The Sioux must be experiencing a touch of diphtheria. The epidemic would have intruded on them through the bands of looters, or maybe the warriors had stolen from someone with the disease.

"How'd he know? Clever medicine man," Slocum moaned out. Had Josiah Jerrold added the herb to his potion knowing it would help quell the effects of diphtheria? That didn't seem likely. He had only added it to change the color.

"Color, gotta get back and change the color of the elixir I mixed up." He sat up and fought down the dizziness. He took a deep breath of the warm night air and felt better. He reached up and pushed his hat back. He had hit his head when he had fallen into the ravine. That explained his disorientation. He focused on what he had to do if he wanted to save Jerrold and Meghan's son and the rest. All the rest.

"Wanna rest," he said, wobbling but holding himself up off the ground with one hand. He wanted to sleep but couldn't.

"Meghan!" He called out the woman's name, not caring if the Indians overheard. She had their horses. They could ride away and leave the Sioux scouting party behind. "Meghan?"

He got to his feet, braced himself for a moment, and then felt a rush of strength pass throughout his shaky legs and arms. His head throbbed where he had smashed it into a rock, but otherwise he was able to keep moving.

Wandering around the arroyo, he began to notice how different this was from where he had left the woman and their horses. This ravine was narrow and not anywhere near as deep. The other had taken most of the drainage from the mesa and poured it over into the prairie. This was likely a feeder rather than the main ravine.

How he had become so disoriented that he had found this rather than returning to the proper arroyo hardly mattered. What did matter was getting the hell away before Big Elk found his powerful medicine stolen. Tromping down the ravine, Slocum occasionally checked the stars for direction. When lacy clouds began masking them, he kept walking, more on intuition than skill.

The arroyo petered out but left Slocum where he could see the black river of the major ravine moving across the mesa. He picked up the pace and was almost running by the time he reached the brink of the deep chasm. This time he approached with more caution, not wanting to take another tumble. A lump as big as a goose egg had sprouted on his forehead, but he ignored the pain when he heard a horse whinny and saw a small, indistinct figure moving to quiet the mare.

His mare. Meghan. He had found the right arroyo this time.

"Where's the rope?" Slocum searched along the edge of the gully, hunting for the rope he had used to climb up.

"John? John! It's in the other direction. You're going the wrong way."

It took a second for him to understand what she meant. He reversed his direction and quickly found the rope dangling from the tree branch. Snaring it, he pulled the rope to him and then slid down fast. His hands burned and his head hurt and he felt great.

"I got the plants," he said, handing Meghan the bags. She took them, hands shaking.

"Oh, John, I hope we're not too late. I have this bad feeling about Frank."

"We'll get back in time. Don't worry."

"I do. Your mare is limping a little."

He remembered how he had met Josiah Jerrold. The snake oil salesman had whipped up liniment for the mare's strained leg.

"You can ride back with the plants."

"You're the one who knows how to mix it. You can take my horse and go."

"I'm not leaving you behind with the Sioux!"

"Then what do we do?"

Slocum found it hard to concentrate but one thing was clear. He wasn't leaving Meghan behind to fend for herself against the Indians. They would be fuming mad when Big Elk told them his medicine plants had been stolen. They were good enough trackers to follow the broad avenue of a trail Slocum had left as he made off with the bags.

"We move," Slocum said decisively. "Now. We get as far away as we can."

"If we go down the trail, they'll find us for sure," Meghan said.

"There's no other choice unless you know a second trail off the mesa." Slocum frowned. "There has to be at least one other, since I doubt the Sioux came up here the same way we did, but they'd find us in a flash if we tried to use it."

"Then let's get started down the trail we know. We might get far enough away so they can't catch us."

Slocum doubted that, but they had to try. He led his horse, noticing the slight limp. He might swap mounts with Meghan since she was lighter and wouldn't put as much strain on the mare's leg as his heavier weight would. But that was for some time in the future. Now they both walked their horses and hoped for the best.

They reached the trailhead and started down, Slocum leading the way. He felt light-headed but sure he could reach the bottom of the trail before sunup. The Sioux braves might be after them then, but they'd have a decent head start.

"What are our chances, John?" Meghan walked along behind him with a light step. In comparison Slocum felt as if he kicked every stone in the trail over the edge and drew attention to himself.

"Good," he said.

"You wouldn't lie, would you? I have this terrible feeling about Frank."

"You're worried, like any good mother," he said. "Frank's held on this long. He can hang on awhile longer."

They walked for another hour, until the first fingers of pink poked up over the horizon. Slocum stopped and looked upward at the mesa rim. A cold lump formed in his gut. He saw movement. It might have been a deer or some other creature out for forage, but then he saw a second indistinct form moving. As the sky lit with dawn, he made out the silhouette.

"We've got to take cover right now," he said. "There are two Sioux braves above us. If they spot us, we're goners."

"Where? We can't just run for it."

"There," he said, seeing a darkness against the cliff face. He led his horse through a rocky patch and behind larger boulders. He stood before a yawning cave mouth. Slocum drew his six-shooter, although he had no chance if the cave was the den for a large carnivore. Three steps convinced him this wasn't a problem. The cave roof tapered down fast, and the rear of the cave was less than fifteen feet back.

Meghan crowded in behind him, leading the horses.

"Will this be big enough?"

"They can't see us from above. The horses can stay in the mouth and we'll have to sprawl out, but there's plenty of room if you don't mind a low ceiling."

"What if they come down the trail? They'll see us for sure!"

"Then we fight," Slocum said. "First, though, we hide. I left Big Elk a bag of his medicine, so they might not be mad enough to risk coming down this side of the mesa."

"What's the risk for them?"

"Disease," Slocum said. "Sentinel Butte isn't that far off. I think Big Elk was collecting the plants because there's diphtheria among his people. It might be quicker and safer for them to find and pick more of the plants than to track us down to get back two stolen bags."

"You really think that?" she asked.

Slocum shrugged. It was possible. All they had to do was wait until they saw how the Sioux reacted. If they didn't follow, Slocum would consider this good rest for both him and his horse a benefit.

He unsaddled his horse to take even more weight off her hoof. He dropped the saddle at the rear of the cave, spread the blanket, and lay back. Immense tiredness washed over him like waves lapping at a lakeshore. Meghan lay beside him, pressing close. He felt her warmth and took strength from her. His arm circled her shoulders so she could snuggle closer, her cheek pressed against his chest.

"We're going to be all right, aren't we?" she asked.

"Frank will be fine," he said, answering her real question. "I won't let anything happen to him."

Slocum half sat up when he felt her fingers working on the buttons of his fly. He started to tell her this wasn't a good idea, not with the Sioux hunting for them, and then all his willpower vanished. She fumbled out his manhood and began stroking along it. In spite of how he felt, Slocum stiffened. Then the bulbous tip disappeared between her questing lips.

He collapsed back and abandoned himself to the sensations gusting through him. Her mouth worked on him slowly at first, then with more insistence. He laced his fingers through her hair, guiding her up and down in a way that aroused him even more.

"You don't have to do this," he said, but the instant the words escaped his lips he knew they were a lie. Meghan had to. And he wanted her to.

Slocum wiggled about a little more and positioned himself so she could take even more of his length into her mouth. He felt her tongue dancing over the tip and then stroking the entire underside as he slid more deeply into her mouth. She used her teeth to stimulate. And her soft lips caressed as she pulled back.

Turning even more, she was able to look at him as she mouthed him. His green eyes met her bright blue ones. He wondered what thoughts were going through her mind. Did she consider this payment for all he had done—or insurance that he would see that her boy survived? As she began turning her head from side to side while he was fully in her mouth, he lost all coherent thought and only experienced.

The delight welled up within him and set him on fire. She sucked loudly. Her cheeks went concave as she worked more avidly on his organ. All Slocum had to do was lie back and let her have her way. But it was a way he wanted to go, too. She began playing with his balls, teasing them with her fingers and occasionally abandoning his fleshy stalk to kiss and lick. Every touch was liquid fire that set his pulse racing just a little faster.

His breathing turned tortured, and he gasped out as he lost control. She continued working on him with her mouth, kissing and licking and touching with only the tip of her tongue until he sank back, drained.

"You knew just what to do," he said. "Just what I needed." He tried to say more, but the thoughts jumbled in his brain and his throat refused to form the words. "Let me rest my eyes. For a moment. Only a moment."

He sank back, his shoulders supported by his saddle. His eyelids drooped, then popped open. He reached for his six-shooter when he saw sunlight angling down into the mouth of the cave. Meghan sat cross-legged beside the horses, staring out away from him.

"You should have woke me up. I must have slept for hours."

"You didn't say how long it would be until the Sioux gave up the hunt for us. I didn't see any reason to wake you until we were sure they'd gone."

"Are they?"

"I don't know. I haven't looked up at the mesa top," she said. "I didn't want them spotting me the way you did them at dawn."

Slocum got to his feet, ducked low because of the cave roof, and worked his way to a spot where he could stand upright. He was just inside the cave, by the horses.

"It's been three hours. If they were coming down the trail, they would have by now."

"Your horse's leg is tender, but I think it'll carry you. We ought to get to town." Her voice was listless.

"What's wrong?"

"Nothing—oh, I don't know. I'm worried about Frank. I'm worried and out here with you and the medicine that might save him and I don't know!" She pulled away from him when he put his hand on her shoulder.

"Time to ride. You take my mare. I'm not leaving you out here in the countryside alone."

"The Sioux won't be a problem," she said. "I don't know about the looters. By now most of them will have moved on or fallen sick with diphtheria."

Slocum hated to admit that her pessimistic view was right, but it carried a note of truth to it. There were only so many farms and ranches to rob. From what Meghan had said about the townspeople, the ones that had survived the epidemic had lit out. Sentinel Butte would be a ghost town by the time the disease had run its course—and Slocum thought it must be close to being at an end. Those that were susceptible had caught it and those, like him and Meghan, who were immune, weren't likely to stay around.

He led the horses back to the trail, then craned his neck around and peered up into the bright Dakota sky. Nowhere along the rim did he catch sight of a brave peering down. If they hadn't taken the trail down by now, they weren't going to. Whether harvesting more of the medicine for Big Elk or simply riding on, the Indians were not a threat.

"Come on, mount up," he said, holding his mare's reins for Meghan. She stepped up easily and led the way down. Slocum found it harder for him to mount her horse. He had forgotten to adjust the stirrups, but that wasn't the problem. His legs were curiously weak.

Rather than dwell on that, Slocum rode the best he could to catch up with her. At the base of the trail, he again looked back to see if they were being followed. As far as he could tell, they were alone in the world. A soft, moist breeze began blowing and clouds built on the horizon.

"We'd better hurry," he told her, "or we'll get caught in a storm."

The storm hit before they were halfway back to Sentinel Butte, but they rode on. They had to. Slocum had to prepare the medicine for those afflicted with the disease.

20

They rode through the pouring rain to the doctor's office. Meghan dismounted and went inside without so much as a word. That suited Slocum. He was having trouble keeping his eyes focused. He had been going too far too long without proper food or sleep, though it had been a delightful moment back in the cave. Still, getting the notion that a Sioux warrior might appear at any instant, knife in hand, had distracted him at every turn. More than this, his mare had been limping.

Slocum stepped down from Meghan's horse and went to examine the mare's leg. While tender, it seemed to be holding up well. With another treatment of Jerrold's curative solution and rest, the horse would be fit enough for the trail in a couple days.

"I'll get some more liniment made up for you," Slocum said, remembering that Jerrold had used the same potion for the horse's leg that had helped the diphtheria victims.

Slocum wiped rain from his eyes, climbed clumsily into the back of the medicine wagon, and dropped his two bags of herbs onto the workbench. The batch of the basic solution he had fixed before had begun to settle a mite. Sediment at the bottom mocked him, leaving behind a color similar to the one he needed the herbs to produce.

He shook up the bottle with the mixture, put in the proper amount—or what he thought was the proper amount—of the herb stolen from Big Elk and held it up. For a moment he couldn't focus his eyes well enough to even see if the color was right. Knowing how important this was, Slocum rummaged about the cluttered interior until he found a coal oil lamp and lit it. This gave him a better chance to study what he had brewed.

The color was off, still too dark and murky. He took a sip and made a face. It didn't taste right, either. Working carefully, hands shaking as he prepared the plant leaves, he added a second pinch to the elixir. This time the color was closer after he shook it up. He took another swig to check. It tasted terrible but about the way Jerrold's had more than a week ago, before they had ridden into town and found an epidemic flourishing.

Slocum sat for a moment, then realized he felt better. Bolstered by the touch of elixir, he took another, then wiped his lips. It wouldn't do if he drank it all himself. There were disease victims that needed saving. He had Frank Mallory to save. He had promised. Besides, what made him feel best of all was triumph. Jerrold might be sick, but his potion would be delivered compliments of John Slocum.

Occasionally taking a swig of his witch's brew to be sure he was on the right track to a proper formulation, Slocum worked until he had used all the plants he had stolen from Big Elk. He was bone tired but felt good otherwise. He had accomplished all he could. Picking up the two jugs of medicine, he swung around and tried to stand. His legs threatened to give out under him, one going out to his right and the other refusing to move at all.

Slocum caught himself, made sure he wasn't going to spill any of the precious fluid, and then made his way to the back of the wagon. The rain pelted down harder than before. He pulled his hat brim lower to shield his eyes, jumped down into the mud, then took both jugs of medicine into the doctor's office.

"Got it," he called into the stillness. No lamps had been lit. The office looked more like a morgue. "Start spooning it out." He put the jugs down on Dr. Wilson's desk and turned, falling into the man's chair. It creaked under Slocum's weight.

"How is everybody?" Slocum fought to focus his eyes again. He saw Meghan across the room, kneeling by Frank. To one side Josiah Jerrold groaned, whether in pain or simply from a fever dream Slocum couldn't tell. The best he could tell, four others were stretched out, having been brought in from the tents outside. "Got enough to go around."

Slocum sat in the chair, feeling as if someone else spoke the words. He floated from his body and looked back at himself in shock. His eyes were sunken and his pallor was that of a blanched carrot. A sudden dazzling lightning bolt lit the interior and then plunged it into utter darkness. Slocum tried to say something more but sank forward, head cradled by his arms on the desk.

"Take this."

"No, no, tastes bad," he heard someone else saying, but the bitter taste on his lips and tongue put the lie to the notion of anyone protesting on his behalf. Slocum's eyes fluttered open, and he saw Meghan holding a spoonful of the medicine. He tried to smile. The small movement of his lips was enough for her to shove in the spoon and dump it. He gagged.

He tried to say something more and then passed out.

Fire. His flesh burned. And he was cold. He shivered and pulled the threadbare blanket around his shoulders. He felt sweat beading his forehead, but he heard perfectly everything going on in the doctor's office.

"Soon. We'll take care of it soon."

"You'll do it right now," Meghan said forcefully. "You won't like it if you don't."

Slocum tried to make out the reply, but the darkness slowly devoured him once more.

"Which is it, son? Are you afraid you'll live, or are you afraid you'll die?"

"Jerrold?" Slocum worked his eyes open to bright sunlight. He was outside in a tent. "You moved me?"

"The air was a bit tight inside, son," Jerrold said. "You knowin' where you are is a good sign. Your old brain's starting to work again. Here, drink this."

Jerrold forced more of the bitter elixir on him.

"I don't have a fever anymore," Slocum said. "But I'm so tired."

"You've earned a good nap. Sleep. Next time when you wake up we'll get some food into you."

"No, no food," Slocum said. The thought of food on his empty belly made him sick. He rolled away and slipped into a soft, quiet sleep.

The beef broth made him gag, but Slocum fought to swallow it all. He didn't know the woman feeding him but thought she might be one of the Cyprians who had so bemused Meghan. A whore doing nurse's work? Slocum had heard of stranger things in his day. Everyone pitched in when disaster struck. At least the folks who were decent did. He wondered how many citizens of Sentinel Butte had simply ridden from town rather than risk the disease, or had taken their wagons and belongings and left after they recovered—even though everyone knew you couldn't get the disease again if you'd had it once.

Slocum frowned as that thought occurred to him. Where had he heard that? He knew men who had contracted cholera more than once. Something didn't add up.

He swallowed more of the broth and felt better for it.

"Where's Meghan? I want to talk to her."

"I don't know any Meghan," the woman said, dishing out more of the broth for Slocum.

"I'd like to talk to Dr. Jerrold then."

"He's around. The epidemic's purty near over," the woman said. "I came into town a day or two ago, and the ones who weren't laid up like you were in a sorry condition. All tired out from fighting the diphtheria. That's what Dr. Jerrold said it was." She spooned in more broth. "He said you were the one that saved most everyone who was left." She glanced in the direction of the shed behind the doctor's office. Slocum turned and got a quick glimpse of it, too.

The shed was gone.

She saw his interest and said, "The undertaker carted them all off and put them in a big pit filled with lime. Ugly. I didn't see it, gettin' to town as late as I did."

"On the stage?"

She nodded. Then she put down the bowl and spoon and stood. "I've got to get over to the general store and help out. It's a shame what happened to Sentinel Butte, but finding a job surely was easy. I worried I'd have to do laundry and sewing, but I have my pick of jobs. Why, I was even offered a job at the bank because I can read and cipher." She picked up the bowl and handed it to Slocum. "You feed yourself all right?"

Slocum allowed as to how he could try. Half-propped up on the cot, he slurped his way to the bottom of the bowl after the woman left. His belly tried to do somersaults, but Slocum held it down. He was as weak as a day-old kitten, but his vision was clear and his other senses as sharp as ever. He heard footsteps coming slowly from behind where he lay.

"Meghan?"

"Sorry, son, I'm not your lady friend." Josiah Jerrold sat on the edge of the cot, tipping it precariously. Both men shifted their weight until an uneasy balance was obtained.

"You're looking like you could whip your weight in wildcats."

"Only if they're small and there aren't more than a dozen or two," Slocum said. He fell silent, waiting for Jerrold to speak. The patent medicine salesman didn't meet his gaze. Slocum knew something unpleasant was about to be laid at his doorstep.

"She's not going to be comin' round, son."

"Meghan? She caught diphtheria?"

"No, she was one of the lucky ones who couldn't get it. You weren't. You came down with a mild case, though."

"I wasn't sick," Slocum protested. "I was only tired."

"Tired and sipping at the concoction you made up?"

"Well, I had to. The taste was as important as the way it looked."

"You didn't know my formula so you matched it with the memory of its taste." Jerrold nodded knowingly. "That's a good thing you didn't burn out your tongue with whiskey years back."

"By sampling the way I did, I kept the symptoms from getting too bad?"

"That seems reasonable to me."

"You're going to have to be wary next time you meet up with Big Elk. I stole the medicine from him."

"Meghan told me the story. Big Elk and me go back a ways. He won't hold it against me, not if I show up with a wagon full of gifts for him and his squaws."

"And?" Slocum prodded.

Jerrold heaved a deep sigh, closed his eyes, then opened them slowly and fixed his rheumy gaze on Slocum.

"She's gone, son. Meghan's gone."

"She died?"

"No, no, not that. She left Sentinel Butte a few days ago."

"I thought I heard her arguing with someone. It seemed real, but I was running a fever."

"You probably heard her and the undertaker. She's got a

mouth on her, that one. He didn't want to tend to business and she insisted."

"Business? Frank?"

Josiah Jerrold nodded sadly. "The boy died right after you whipped up the last batch of potion. His poor little body had been put under too much strain for too long. It wasn't your fault the potion didn't work for him, because it did for just about everyone else. He was already more dead than alive, and nothing would have saved him. But she didn't think so."

"She blamed me?"

Jerrold looked away and said, "She made the undertaker bury her son next to his pa. Not many who died later on in the epidemic got planted out there in the cemetery proper. Most were tossed into a lime pit and then plowed under."

"Where did she go?"

"Wouldn't say, but there wasn't anything holding her here, unless you count her hatred for you. It's a good thing you were already sick or she might have gunned you down."

"I did the best I could."

"Wasn't enough. She said you promised. No man can keep a promise if God's not willing to go along. Anyhow, she got herself a buckboard and drove out of town."

"Which direction?"

"Don't ask, son. Don't ask." Jerrold thought for a moment and said, "You're held in somewhat higher esteem by Marshal Sully and a couple of his boys. The marshal said to thank you for savin' him and for you to get the hell out of the territory. He doesn't want to see you again."

"I seem to have that effect on a lot of people."

"Not on everyone. When you're feeling chipper, if you want, you can ride along with me a spell. Don't know where I'm heading but it's away from the Dakotas. I might not be as pretty as your lady friend, but then I don't have a six-gun that I'd want to use on you if you turn your back."

Slocum sank back onto the cot, exhausted in both body and mind.

"I'll fetch you some water. You drink on it as much as you can. That'll get your strength up. Consider partnering up with me, at least for a town or two. We make a great team, Slocum." Josiah Jerrold left the tent. Slocum watched his silhouette cross the canvas and disappear.

He lay back and closed his eyes, trying to get everything square in his mind. He might ride with Jerrold, for a while. Sleep slowly possessed him again, and John Slocum dreamed of a beautiful woman with bright blue eyes and a captivating smile and hair darker than midnight.

When he awoke he knew it was all a dream. Only a dream.

Watch for

SLOCUM AND THE SECOND HORSE

376th novel in the exciting SLOCUM series
from Jove

Coming in June!

DON'T MISS A YEAR OF

Slocum Giant
by
Jake Logan

Slocum Giant 2004:
Slocum in the Secret Service

Slocum Giant 2005:
Slocum and the Larcenous Lady

Slocum Giant 2006:
Slocum and the Hanging Horse

Slocum Giant 2007:
Slocum and the Celestial Bones

Slocum Giant 2008:
Slocum and the Town Killers

Slocum Giant 2009:
Slocum's Great Race

penguin.com/actionwesterns